MW01659541

Buried

A 30th Street Fiction Anthology

Other 30th Street Fiction Anthologies

Proof

Evidence? Alcohol content? A product sample? In this short story collection, proof can be that ghosts, zombies, and aliens are real or long kept secrets finally see the light of day.

Flight

To flee? To fly? A set of stairs?
In this collection of short stories, flight means rockets, space ships, and thrills. It means refusing to settle and finding the courage to change.

Broken

A record? A vow? A bone? A dream?
In this collection of short stories, broken means betrayal, fixing instead of buying new, and the place where ordinary meets mystery and fantasy.

Buried

A 30th Street Fiction Anthology

Stories by Caitlin Berve, Laura Blegen, Richard M. Hamp, Jon Logan Hart, Kate Jonuska, Jessica Lavé, Ian K. Long, and Juliana Rew

Edited by Caitlin Berve, Lezly Harrison & Juliana Rew

Introduction by Lezly Harrison

30th Street Press

Boulder

Broken: A 30th Street Fiction Anthology / Caitlin Berve, Laura Blegen, Richard M. Hamp, Lezly Harrison, Jon Logan Hart, Kate Jonuska, Jessica Lavé, Ian K. Long, & Juliana Rew

Copyright © 2023 Caitlin Berve, Laura Blegen, Richard M. Hamp, Lezly Harrison, Jon Logan Hart, Kate Jonuska, Jessica Lavé, Ian K. Long, & Juliana Rew

All rights reserved. No part of this publication may be reproduced, distributed, or transmitted in any form or by any means, including photocopying, recording, AI training, or other electronic or mechanical methods, without the prior written permission of the publisher, except in the case of brief quotations embodied in critical reviews and certain other noncommercial uses permitted by US copyright law.

All characters appearing in this work are fictitious and were created without the use of AI. Any resemblance to real persons, living or dead, is purely coincidental.

Published 2023 by 30th Street Press
30thstreetpress.com

Edited by: Caitlin Berve, Lezly Harrison, and Juliana Rew
Cover design: Kate Jonuska
Interior design: Jessica Lavé and Caitlin Berve

ISBN 979-8-9876693-0-3

1. Fiction—Speculative Fiction. 2. Mainstream Fiction. 3. Fantasy and Science Fiction.

First Edition Printing
Printed in the United States of America

Contents

Introduction:
Buried in Words

Lezly Harrison

BURIED IN ME was a writer. Maybe there's one buried in you, too. You might not know it yet, or maybe you just found out, or maybe you've known for a long time or your entire life, but from the first time you read that old axiom, "You can't edit a blank page," you've been shoveling words onto the page by the pile.

Big words. Little words. Wrong words. Superfluous words. Awkward words—that was awkward. Funny words. Boring words. Words that don't make any sense. Words that conjure too many scents. Words you wrote that no one will read. Words you wish that no one had read.

You pull some of your best words from your digital mound and sculpt them into something you hope is fun and interesting and give your piece to trusted family and friends and the responses are more than you'd hoped for! These are great words, they tell you. Moving. Stirring. But you know they're not. They're not bad words; they're just not great.

You're sure, though, that somewhere in that electronic heap, there's a body of work worth digging out, but exhuming a body isn't for the squeamish. While your family and friends were well-meaning, you need someone who wants you to be a better writer more than they care about your feelings.

You need a critique group.

One of the best ways to find a critique group is to talk to other writers, but all the writers I knew were technical writers. I had story ideas outlined in spiral notebooks along with first chapters and short story starts—all longhand! But I'd never seriously attempted to craft an entire story with a cast of characters and a plot with a beginning, a middle, and an end. So, I did what any techie would do and looked on social media, where I found three critique groups near me. I visited all three, stuck with two for a while and eventually settled on just one, 30th Street Fiction, but most of the members in my group participate in multiple groups.

I also searched for writers' organizations and found several along the front range. Many offer free workshops and events where you can learn more about the art of writing and meet local writers, and often their websites list critique groups who are accepting members.

Generally, I've found writers to be encouraging of others' craft. We want to see other authors pen good stories, because who doesn't love a good story, but also it reinforces our confidence that we can write a good story, too.

Once you find the right crew for your mission, the messy work of digging up your body just got easier. As you unearth your words from the pile onto the page, your writing group assists with applying flesh to the bones of your story, of fashioning characters with depth and heart, of forming plots with intrigue that engage the mind. In turn, you'll help your fellow writers create their stories, offering you an entirely different perspective and learning opportunity on writing.

Besides a team you can trust, you'll want a group who has a variety of skills.

My group has a couple of experts in grammar, punctuation, and usage, and we have members who argue various manuals of style. One member, who shall remain nameless, lets the praise goes to his head, is especially good at giving a macro-assessment and pointing out the overall great thing or not-so-great thing about the piece. Besides individual comments, group discussions often reveal flaws in a premise or holes in a plot. Conversely, in their own stories, my fellow writers have provided wonderful examples of how to develop living people on the page, a skill my paper doll characters hope

I improve upon. And while some of us turn out an exceptional phrase on occasion, we have a few members who are masters at it. We all have weaknesses to improve, but we also have strengths to offer.

Criticism of something you've put your entire being into can be hard to take, even when offered in the spirit of progress, but as you excavate your body of work and help your fellow writers mine theirs, a bond of trust and respect develops. And more. These people have become your friends.

So, six years ago when someone in group suggested a collaborative effort, an anthology of short stories revolving around a common theme, we were all excited to contribute, to work together and craft individual stories each with a piece of our hearts. *Buried* is the fourth anthology in our collection and we hope you enjoy digging through our words and getting to know the bodies we created.

~ Lezly Harrison

Scarlet Secrets and Sienna Sands

Caitlin Berve

WE GATHERED BECAUSE the desert called to us. Through the grittiness of sand in our mouths. Through the scent of creosote and hot dunes. Through the heat of unfiltered sunlight and the sensation of open, empty possibilities.

We arrived from tundras, tropics, and oceans. We scaled mountains and waded rivers. We left behind property, careers, and lovers. All because the desert called.

We are made from her rocks, her breeze, her precious, precious water. She loved us, cared for us, and one by one, wished us well as we ventured into the world, living as we pleased until she called us home.

Ceaseless winds and infrequent flash floods have reshaped her, but the desert is still our mother and still our home. So we rebuilt the worn-away structures and carved out new spaces for our houses. We gathered in towns, segregated by the kinds of secrets we kept for her, and we waited for her direction.

One by one, her instructions arrived. One by one, we collected more secrets, adding more grains of sand to our land. He was another secret to collect.

He drove into our town's two-pump gas station with his head high, confident. Red dust clung to his white Mercedes-Benz sedan, dulling the paint's sparkle, marking the vehicle's journey through our desert hills. As he filled the car with premium gas, he noticed one of our girls—home from college for spring break—getting gas and gave her a white-toothed grin that made butterflies flutter in our stomachs. We all felt her blush blossom across our cheeks.

He squeezed the faded gas pump extra hard, flexing his toned muscles and making the three-quarter sleeve of his fitted Henley t-shirt rise just enough to show the tip of a thin, red scar. He wore the top three buttons loose to show off his shaved, toned chest. When he bent over to pick up an empty coke bottle, the fit of his jeans suggested they'd been tailored just for him. He used the bottle to stuff the trash deeper into the trash can and stop it from blowing out.

We wanted to like him. We wanted to befriend and welcome him, just like the people in the other towns he was "passing through". But the desert air settled, warning us to be still. To watch. To look closer.

When he slipped the gas nozzle back into its holder, the pump slid out and nearly crashed to the ground before he caught it. He cursed under his breath and peered into the holder.

Our girl giggled and shouted over to him. "You have to push it over the lip until the nozzle catches." He did as she suggested, and we all felt the familiar click of the metal nozzle catching.

Charisma rolled off him in a cloud of intoxicating cologne as he sauntered over to our girl and said, "You seem to know your way around. What's your favorite place to eat here?"

"Jacy's Deli," she said and tucked a loose strand of long hair behind her ear. Sun-bleached highlights shimmered like gold in her black braid, and the metallic letters of her college initials glittered on her v-neck t-shirt. "Just keep going down Main Street. It's the red adobe building on your left."

"Thank you." He smiled again. His eyes flitted to her well-loved yet deteriorating Subaru Outback with the college parking sticker filling the lower corner of the driver's side windshield. For a second, the gleam in his eyes became a cold assessment of its contents. "I see your suitcase in the back seat. I'm guessing you're home from college for the summer. How about I buy your first lunch back in town?"

"That's nice of you, but I'm sure my mom will have something waiting for me."

"Oh, come on." He waved down the street. "Haven't you been craving one of Jacy's sandwiches this whole semester?"

She bit her lip, and we knew what she was thinking. This wasn't the dangerous big city she'd moved to for school. This was the small town she grew up in. She knew every shadow and secret and felt the eyes of the elderly gas clerk and young customer buying gum on her through the dusty windows of the convenience store. She knew we'd watch out for her.

Seeing her start to cave, he said, "I'll tell you a secret." A hot, desert breeze arrived to scoop up his next words. "I hate eating alone."

The breeze ruffled our girl's hair and we all felt the subtle presence of the desert like a comforting squeeze on our shoulder from a loved one. Her shoulders relaxed and her eyes locked onto his.

"Okay," she said. "Follow me." They each climbed in their own car.

As she drove, our girl rolled down her window and let the hot breeze tease her hair and tickle her cheek like a mother's kiss. We knew that meant the desert was watching over our girl and us.

We all felt his arrival in town and at the deli. Children of the desert, caretakers of her sands, she alerts us to all new arrivals. And we knew what that breeze and promise of a secret meant. Deserts like ours collect secrets. When people whisper them into the winds or scream them into their pillows, the air currents of the world sweep up the secrets and deposit them in its deserts. Here, secrets are broken down into grains of sand and scattered among our lands to never again coalesce and betray or weigh down their bearers.

His "secret"—not wanting to eat alone—was the tip of the massive iceberg of violent, deadly secrets he thrived on. But icebergs don't last long in the heat, and the desert wouldn't have led him to our little town if she didn't want his secrets—and ability to make more—buried in her sands where they couldn't do more damage.

He followed our girl up the steps to the only maroon adobe structure in town. Above the door in turquoise letters was *Jacy's Deli*. They were greeted by a tinkling bell and massive, lighted menu above the cash register so faded that our girl had to list most of the options for him.

"I'll have your favorite," he said and gently squeezed her upper arm to guide her to the side. His hand lingered a little too long and his fingers flexed when he released her the way a cat flexes her nails after losing her prey. We wanted to hiss at his predatory movements and promise of violence, but we held our tongue and waited for the desert's signal.

"Two Jacy Secret Specials," she announced to the cashier, a teenage boy whose cheeks flushed when he made eye contact with our girl. Even though he'd grown since she'd last seen him—his limbs were still lanky and not yet filled with the muscles of puberty—he lumbered about, unsure of his new size.

"That's not on the menu." The outsider pointed to the faded sign.

"That's what makes it the *secret* special." She smiled then turned to the cashier. "And two waters, please."

The young cashier's voice cracked when he said, "Coming right up."

As the outsider looked down at the screen to pay, our cashier gave her a quick nod before completing the transaction. Then he whistled his way to the back. Normally, he'd have stuttered at interacting with a girl like her—older, sexier, bolder—but today he gained confidence from the desert's directions, as we all did.

"Booth or table?" she asked.

And the outsider answered, "Booth. Away from the window. It's too hot in the sun."

"Of course." She guided him to the back booth. The one with silver duct tape holding the side of the maroon seat together and a deep gouge in the center of the black table. "So why don't you like to eat alone?" she asked once they were settled with his back to the window and face in shadow.

"Food doesn't taste as good unless it's shared with someone special." He gave her a lazy, slow wink.

She raised an eyebrow at him, and we rolled our eyes.

"Ok, I moved a lot as a kid, so I ate a bunch of lunches alone before I made friends."

"For some reason, I find it hard to believe you had trouble making friends." She smiled. It was genuine. She still wanted to like him.

He laughed.

"Order up!" called the teenage boy from the front.

"I got it." He held up his hand and stood quickly.

We all watched him stride down the aisle and carefully pull a small syringe from his pocket. Smoothly, he squeezed a clear liquid into one glass as he reached for the tray. Our girl winced with the rest of us, wondering how many others he'd used that trick on. By the time he returned to the table, both waters appeared undisturbed. This was all the proof we needed, yet the desert winds still rose, whipping back and forth until dust devils grew all over town. The desert had spoken; we had another secret—and secret maker—to take care of.

When he set the tray down on their table, our cashier called back to him, "Forgot the napkins," and waved a handful above the counter. The outsider placed the drugged water glass and a sandwich in front of our girl before quickly striding to grab the napkins.

The tiniest bit of desert sand fell from the ceiling, marking the drugged glass and dissolving inside it. With a slight tremble in her fingers, our girl switched the waters before the outsider turned back toward her. Despite the desert's aid, her palms began to sweat and we all felt their stickiness. Collectively, we took a breath as he returned, dropped the flimsy napkins on the table, and slid into his seat.

Our girl swirled her water, making the ice cubs clink against the glass and the liquid almost spill over the top before smiling coyly and taking a large gulp. Her tremble was gone. He grinned, still thinking he was the predator in our town, while the rest of us smirked, knowing better.

She pointed to his full glass. "Aren't you thirsty? You need to stay hydrated. The desert sucks the water right out of your skin."

He tilted his head back and poured a third of the water into his mouth, crunching and swallowing the ice that came with it. "Your turn."

She took another large gulp. Together we felt the sweet relief of a cool drink on a hot day and the sensation of water on our tongues. The desert was telling us to have patience. To let the desert's spell and the drugs he'd tried to give our girl do their job. To wait just a little longer to make our move.

"That's not really your secret, though, is it? I bet you tell all the cute girls you hate eating alone." She let her eyelids flutter as she spoke. We felt the thrill bubbling within her. The real secret was coming and we couldn't wait to taste it.

"It's still a secret if only a few people know, isn't it?" he asked.

"Oh, I bet more than a few know that one." She ran her finger down the side of her glass, collecting the beads of water, and licked the liquid off the tip of her finger.

His eyes locked onto her mouth as he said, "None that are still around, though."

We grew uncomfortable under his gaze and squirmed with our girl.

He shook his head and pointed to the sandwiches. "Let's eat." They devoured the food in silence, both ravenous for a different kind of meal.

Finished, she slumped back in her seat and stretched as if tired, a better actress than any of us thought. "Tell me a real secret. One no one else knows." She stifled a fake yawn, and we leaned forward—at our desks, in our fields, against our kitchen counters—eager for the answer.

He yawned back at her. "A real secret? Sometimes I like it a little rough." This wasn't exactly a secret, but it wasn't the kind of thing a person would say to a stranger, either. His filter was slipping alongside his consciousness, but he continued to hold onto his charm.

"That's closer, but it's still not a real secret." As he faded, our girl sat up a bit straighter and leaned across the counter. "How about I start?" she said, "This is my first time." She winked.

He chuckled in satisfaction and mumbled something with the words "always remember."

She nudged his foot, and we all felt the pressure of him against our toes. We were so close. "Your turn. Tell me a dark one."

He roused himself somewhat, sat up a bit more, and reached for her hand, coming up short. "I devour girls like you." The light left his eyes, consumed by the darkness that filled them, revealing the monster behind the façade. He clacked his teeth and we were struck with the image of a coyote tearing into a rabbit.

There it was. We shivered with glee. His secret had been spoken, and like our girl, we knew he meant it figuratively and literally. A month ago in our sister town, nestled in the white desert sands that glittered like snow, a girl had gone missing, and only her upper half had been found, gnawed on. Our desert had been too shocked to stop him then. But now that he'd found his way back, a flash flood conveniently washed out the main highway, forcing him onto the road that led to our little town, where the sands are a brilliant rusty red, capable of securing heavier, darker secrets than the fine white dunes and their caretakers.

Our girl also shivered at his answer, an involuntary shudder of excitement, and we all whispered the next words with her.

"Here, we feed on secrets," she said to the outsider. "They fill out our flesh like calories and warm our souls like the sun warms the sand. And we're going to spill your secrets all over our land, so they can feed our plants and animals and bring more life to our red desert. So, tell us another secret."

We spoke too eagerly, with too much passion for a girl succumbing to drugs. His eyes widened and he sat up too quickly. His tan skin turned ashen, and he slumped back into the booth. "Whaaa did ooo dooo?" he slurred.

"Nothing. You just drank out of the wrong glass. The same way you picked the wrong girl and stopped in the wrong town."

A fierce gust ripped through our town, carrying the scent of wildfire smoke, and we rose. The teenage boy stepped out from behind the counter. At the same time, the door opened, and single file, we, the people of the desert, strode down the aisle and gathered around him and our girl.

"Whooo yooouu?" the outsider asked and swatted at our hands with more force and strength than we expected. Pushing us away, he half-slid, half-tumbled from the booth. He kicked at our advance and flailed his arms, so we waited for his movements to become weaker as he faded in and out of the dark place he'd sent so many girls before. Then we grasped his arms and pulled him onto a backboard, used for secrets and injuries, and lashed him to it.

We followed our girl to a waiting pickup truck. She hopped in the back with the outsider, who continued mumbling. When everyone else was settled, she rapped on the sun-bleached hood. The nervous sweat had completely dried from her palms and anticipation made us all giddy.

Our convoy of worn, faded vehicles followed the truck to the base of the mesa overlooking our dusty little town. Quail skittered in front of us beneath the scrub brush when our girl and the cashier hopped out and began to lead the way up the well-worn trail to the top. As the sun beat down on the back of our necks and blinded anyone who glanced our way, we hiked up the soft trail. Curious lizards on hot rocks and a lone coyote in the shade watched. Only a few remained in town, monitoring the little kids and main road for any more “guests” sent our way, but they were still privy to the scene on the mesa.

We carried the outsider strapped to the board and our thighs burned with the weight of his secrets. By the time we reached the flattened area at the top, sweat rolled down all of our necks.

A ring of well-watered, thick, thorny scrub brush and trees provided privacy, and the sun lessened in intensity, giving a bit of respite from the heat. To honor our girl’s first time luring such a secret, she was first to enter the clearing. A square, sandstone obelisk rose from the center of the vegetation’s ring. A desert breeze swirled to remove a thick coat of sand from the structure.

Carved into the obelisk in the language of the desert was the story of how our desert created us, cared for us, and ground the secrets of the world into grains of sand, burying them forever in her flesh and destroying the monsters sent to us. Our girl pushed hard to slide the top off the obelisk along tracks worn by generations of our people.

Inside a single, thin, obsidian spike rose from the center of the base. The floor sloped into four long drains that led to the four directions. We lowered the outsider and freed his bonds. “No.” He again swatted at our hands and tried to stand.

“Away,” he mumbled, unable to fight us off the same way his victims had failed to escape his hunger.

As one, our strongest lifted the outsider from the ground, twitching and writhing with all the strength he had left: not much. We showed him the same mercy he showed the other girls and impaled him on the obsidian spike. His eyes widened at the shock and he stilled. We stepped back and shielded our eyes. A scorching ray of sunlight flooded the box, turning all traces of moisture into a mist that rose and coalesced into a single, small rain cloud. His precious water would not go to waste.

Our girl, with help from the teenage cashier, pushed the top of the obelisk closed.

We smiled. For an instant, we were one with everyone who carried a part of the outsider’s monstrous secrets. We took a deep breath and slid that weight from their shoulders onto ours. As we exhaled, that weight shifted from us to the body in the sandstone tomb. We all listened as the base of the obelisk shifted back and forth, grinding the body of secrets within into sand that spilled out of the four holes.

Our smile widened as relief cascaded through us. Our shoulders relaxed. Our jaw unclenched. Our stomach knots unraveled. And everyone who carried a part of the outsider’s secrets relaxed with us, feeling that weight lifted from their shoulders. The wind rose, collected our and his secret and scattered the red grains.

As one, we bowed in the direction of our sister town and the string of victimized towns beyond it, turned, and hiked down the mountain. Our collective consciousness faded into the background, always present, yet inactive until the desert called upon us again.

We are her guardians, born from drops of moonlight sinking into her fertile veins. We are her blades, honed in the relentless heat. We are her oasis, life in the center of what others perceive to be a barren wasteland. We are the keepers of her mysteries, secrets buried long ago because they were deemed too dangerous, too powerful, too catastrophic, too catalyzing.

We welcome the world's secrets. We use the scent of creosote and hot dunes to take that weight. We use the heat of unfiltered sunlight and the sensation of open, empty possibilities to bury those scarlet secrets in our sienna sands.

The Warning Buoy

Jon Logan Hart

STOCKWELL FLICKED HIS lighter and the sparks strobed the cab of his truck as he bumped along the dirt road in the country-black night. Glancing into the rearview mirror, he watched the plume of dust glowing red from his tail lights.

Wait until dark. Then get here. Don't call me on my cell. Keep yours turned off. Better. Leave your phone at home.

That was all he had said. Who the fuck sets up a rendezvous in a pasture at night? *Only Carl.* Stockwell's heart fluttered and his breathing got shallow. "Don't have a panic attack now," he whispered to himself. He'd missed last month's truck payment and didn't have the money for the next. He'd heard nothing back from Texas State about that posting for a menial grad student job. He wasn't sure how long it would take for the finance goons to send the repo men.

Not having a vehicle in Texas was like losing your legs.

The familiar tightening rose in his torso, gripping his heart. He tried that idiotic breathing exercise the doctor had gone on and on about. *In through the nose slowly. Hold it. Exhale.* Something that only comes naturally with a cigarette. *A cigarette.* He took in a deep breath. Smoking and whiskey were the cures for anxiety attacks. Problem was, the cures didn't last and the hangovers were becoming more brutal.

He'd needed both, last weekend when the martinet in charge of the conference had canceled his panel appearance. Being on that panel would have put him in front of all the movers and shakers in the Catastrophic Impact field. "Your presentation skills are wonderful," said the woman with the over-sized glasses, "but your paper is full of wild—though *interesting*—speculations. And we don't see that you've put the *work* into backing up these new theories with evidence."

Stockwell moved his lips and whispered out his reply as his headlights caught cows' heads poked through the barbed-wire fence as they munched on the sweet grass in the drainage ditch.

He'd pleaded to that conference tinpot admin, "But that's the point! The Younger Dryas impact wiped the slate clean. The global flood eliminated everything. It atomized advanced ancient civilizations. Atlantis was swamped by sea levels that rose hundreds of meters in a few hours. Plato was *right* when he wrote of Atlantis sinking into the sea 12,800 years ago. That's exactly when the comet hit. *Think.* All the flood myths from all over the world. Where did they come from? Were they all myths? No. They are *memories*. Handed down from generation to generation."

The conference chair once again adjusted the eyeglasses that were too big for her. Stockwell wanted to smack them off her face. "The consensus among most *credentialed* scientists is . . ." It was always the same blather. They wouldn't listen. Allow him to present his ideas. If he'd finished his PhD, these mediocrities would have cared. They'd have respected him. Because then, like all of them, he'd be *credentialed.*

"Your 'consensus' is bullshit," he whispered bitterly to the shade-memory of the woman as he bounced along the corduroyed road of packed dirt. His front right tire bottomed out into a pothole. "Shit." There goes the alignment. His truck was about to be repossessed, his career was in ashes and what was he doing? Meeting Carl in a fucking pasture at midnight.

He passed Carl's low-slung ranch house. The feeble porch light glowed salmon in the rust-colored Texas dust.

Go past the house and through the cemetery. You'll find me on the edge of the east pasture.

Unlighted, the cemetery at night looked like something from Dante, with neglected white headstones sticking out from the ground in all sorts of crazy angles, like jagged teeth from an old fossil.

Rattling over the cattle guard, he entered the farm. It was 4,000 acres, but Carl always called it "the farm."

About 200 yards distant, well into the pasture, he saw the faint glow from a large white canvas tent. It looked like an archeological dig site. He parked at the barbed-wire fence and after killing the engine he grabbed the bottle of rye and slammed the door shut. He stopped and reached back into the open window for the pack of cigarettes. Leaning against the door, he tapped one out and ran it under his nose, drinking in the sweet, incense-like smell. Sparking the lighter, which caught this time, he took a big pull, filling his lungs. The nicotine kicked in and he instantly felt better, the anxiety loosening its grip and descending back into its hiding place deep inside.

His boots crunched on the gravel up to the place where the wire had been cut and then looped around the fenceposts, creating a make-shift gate.

Approaching the tent, he shouted his presence and then pulled open the flap.

"Get in here and close it," said Carl.

Carl dumped whatever was in his tin coffee cup into the dust. "Thanks for bringing the rye."

Stockwell handed him the bottle. "That's thirty-five dollars I don't have. Sip it, please."

A single kerosene lantern on a crate inside the large, rectangular tent created a strangely alien scene as its trembling flame illuminated a jagged tear in the moon-like crust that was the pasture after a month without rain.

"Meteorite?" Stockwell pulled again on his cigarette. "That couldn't wait until morning?"

Carl shook his head. "It's not what you think."

Stockwell gestured to the tent. "You erect this yourself?"

Carl nodded impatiently, raked back the remaining wisps of his gray hair, and then took a gulp of the rye. "Couldn't risk showing this to anyone but you. At least for now. Raising the tent took me all afternoon." He took another expensive swallow and smiled. "Remember this tent?"

Stockwell nodded. It felt like yesterday. "The Derinkuyu dig in Turkey."

Carl ran his hand along the dirty canvas, as though stroking a lover. "My biggest discovery."

God, he could be so insufferable.

Carl had placed two folding chairs on either side of the crate on which the lantern rested. A shovel was perched against one of the chairs.

Carl grabbed the shovel and tossed it onto the dirt. "You'll want to sit."

Stockwell looked for another glass but saw only the dented metal cup Carl was gesturing with.

Carl shook his head. "I don't know how I was so lucky. It could've landed anywhere."

"What? Part of an airplane? Space junk?"

"I saw the streak. I just happened to be pulling up. I'd been shuttling boxes to my new condo in Austin. You've got to see it, by the way. Twentieth floor. Breathtaking views."

"Waiting on my invitation." That was too sarcastic. Especially when Stockwell needed Carl's goodwill. While one more summer as Carl's TA would be humiliating for a thirty-five-year-old failed PhD candidate, it would pay the past-due bills and save the truck. "Congrats on the new place. Money from your latest book?"

Carl nodded. "Nearly a million copies across all platforms. And still going. I was supposed to leave for a speaking tour next week. I'll have to postpone that now. This is *that* big."

Carl at his most annoying, obliviously obnoxious. Rubbing in his success with one simple sentence. "This is bigger than your book on the Younger Dryas Impact Hypothesis?"

"Yes, of course," Carl answered impatiently.

I came up with that theory. I presented it to you as my dissertation topic. The dissertation I never finished because you suddenly had to fly to New York for a three-minute Good Morning USA interview, leaving me high and dry to get gutted by the hacks on the review committee. I needed you. I wasn't ready to face them on my own. I went down in flames and your only advice afterward was to "give it another go next year after more research.

Carl held out the mug. "Have yourself a drink."

Reliving the dissertation episode always made Stockwell go cold. He wrapped his hand around the neck of the bottle. "That theory." His grip tightened. He felt he could crack it off. "Was mine."

Carl never read people well. "Tom Stockwell, if I've told you once, I've told you a thousand times. You're brilliant with your ideas and inspirations. But science is the sweat and tears and disappointments of hard, sustained work. The day-to-day grind under the brutal sun. *Anyone* can come up with ideas."

Stockwell's grip was ratcheted tight like a vice. The arrogance. The pomposity. "I was there with you, at Derinkuyu."

Carl was exasperated. "For a few days out of a nine-month dig! You can't just have ideas. You've got to back them up with the actual hard work of testing them, investigating, finding what's likely to be true. Or not. Otherwise it's speculation suited only for—a—" He searched for the right word. "—A novel."

Cold sweat ran down Stockwell's forehead. He wiped it out of his eyes with his free hand. "It's all so easy for you to say. You've got tenure. Royalties. I have to scratch out a living doing odd jobs. While *your* speculations are selling well, based on my ideas."

Carl waved, as though shooing a fly from his face. "Stockwell, here is your chance. What I'm about to show you is, I believe, the most important artifact discovered, ever."

Stockwell nodded and swallowed down the rage with a sip of rye. He had to keep his head. Keep his wits. *Your rages are always your undoing. Keep it together.* Whatever was in this trench had to be something.

Carl put his hand on Stockwell's shoulder, his ice blue eyes almost sympathetic and understanding. "And you and I. *Together*. We can figure this out." He gave Stockwell a patronizing pat.

Stockwell took another swallow and nodded. "When did it hit?"

"Night before last."

"Why didn't you call me then?"

Carl gripped his chin. "I had no idea what I was dealing with. It was this bizarre thing. It shouldn't be here in one piece. It shouldn't be here at all—why didn't it burn up in the atmosphere?"

Stockwell felt a swell of pride to be in on this secret unknown by anyone else in the world. Like he was in one of Carl's lectures back in his undergrad days. Mesmerized as Carl relived his discoveries. He remembered the thrill when Carl had taken him on as a grad student. Because he knew working for the successful and energetic Carl would guarantee a fast ascent in the academic world.

Stockwell refilled the tin cup. The rye looked like molten amber in the lantern light. He took another swallow, enjoying the satisfying burn.

Carl carefully removed a tarp that had been perched over a sawhorse at the end of the gash in the dirt. “It gives me chills to think I might have missed this. Had I not seen the streak in the sky, this gash would have been washed over in the winter rains and I’d never have made the discovery.”

Carl grabbed the lantern and handed it to Stockwell. He then dragged the crate into the center of the tent.

Next, he reached cautiously into the trench and pulled out a black orb, about the size of a bowling ball. “This is exactly as I found it.”

“What the—” Stockwell’s jaw fell open. “There’s no way that could have survived as a perfect sphere burning through the atmosphere.”

As he said that, the shine on the ball evaporated, leaving a singularity—a bowling ball-sized sphere of black emptiness resting in Carl’s hands. Stockwell felt he could put a finger into it, as though it were a porthole, or a portal to . . . what? Another dimension? The other side of the galaxy? That *was* strange. There had to be a reasonable explanation. All he said, though, was, “What the hell is that?” as he reached out tremulously, suddenly feeling like Adam on the ceiling of the Sistine Chapel.

Carl extended his hands. “Hold it.”

Stockwell was surprised he was afraid. That made zero sense. While unsure of whether the ancient, advanced human civilizations were home-grown or not, this little black ball seemed to be showing them that alien *somethings* were involved. And that left Stockwell oddly deflated.

Stockwell reached out and before Carl placed the orb into his cupped hands, the shine returned to the ball.

"Go ahead," said Carl. "You're not taking communion."

It was much heavier than he'd anticipated. A high-voltage electric current jolted down his spine as Stockwell ran his fingers over the lacquered surface, feeling no resistance or friction at all. The orb was cold as ice inside a tent that had to be ninety. "How did you get it so clean?"

"That's just it." Carl stepped gingerly over to the crate. "This is exactly how I found it."

"You had no idea what it was. It could've been a bomb. Or some weapon that fell out of orbit."

Carl nodded. "When I saw this hit, I grabbed my Geiger counter and spectrometer and ran out into the field. The trench was still smoking, but there was nothing bad coming from the object, no radiation, no gas. I dribbled water onto it and it rolled off. It was cool to the touch and, as you see, a perfect sphere, smooth as glass."

Stockwell knew he would have done the same thing. "But there is no way that thing could have survived as a perfect sphere burning through the atmosphere. Perhaps it was a part of a larger ship, or buried within a small asteroid?"

"I don't know. But its spherical perfection is the least of what makes it exceptional." Carl checked his watch. "And if it keeps the same cadence, you're about to see something you could never have imagined."

Carl placed the sphere on the crate. The black orb had the liquid luminescence of crude oil, as though it should dissolve, sticky and viscous, into a pool.

Stockwell tapped out another Marlboro.

Carl turned the knob on the kerosene lamp and blackness closed in.

Stars of light began, one by one, to flicker on the surface of the orb. Yellow, blue, red, orange, white. Some were tiny, some large. The largest star, a brilliant red, shimmered and pulsed.

"Look up," said Carl quietly.

Stockwell gasped. "Wha—" The lights from the orb projected onto the canvas all around them, like in a planetarium.

Stockwell reached for the much-used cup and took a gulp. He was watching something from a dream. This artifact had journeyed many light years, potentially tens of thousands. And it was *communicating*. "Oh, my god. My god . . ."

In the dim starlight, he could see Carl turning this way and that, as if taking it all in for the first time.

"I know," said Carl. "The last two nights, at midnight. It's done this." He pointed to the opposite side of the tent.

Stockwell took another gulp, draining the mug. He set it down, pushed back his chair and stood. "Orion?"

"Uh huh."

Stockwell walked over and tried to touch the stars but he blocked the light projecting from the sphere and saw only his shadow. Backing into his chair, he looked again at the pattern on the canvas. "Holy shit. That *is* Orion. And the pulsing big red star, that's—"

Carl's voice trembled with excitement. He reached for the cup and gestured. "Betelgeuse. The red super-giant star in the most recognizable constellation in the sky."

Carl poured a finger of rye into their shared cup.

And then, as if a switch had been flicked, the lights on the canvas vanished.

"Just like the last two nights." Carl relighted the lamp. The crystals on the sphere were dark, lifeless. Then, as though a magnet inside the ball had been pulled away, they all slipped off and skittered onto the crate, some sliding through the slats onto the dirt. Stockwell tentatively extended a finger to the sparkling artifacts on the crate.

"Go ahead," said Carl. "Pick one up."

Stockwell picked up a blue crystal and flicked his lighter. Holding it in front of the flame, another jolt of electricity shot up his spine. "Are these?"

Carl nodded, smiling broadly. "I checked them this morning. One hundred percent crystalized carbon, with trace elements added for color."

Stockwell dropped the sapphire-colored crystal and reached for the large red one and held it in front of his lighter's flame. "*Diamonds?* You've got to be kidding me. Diamonds take months to synthesize and need all that heat and pressure."

"The heat and pressure found near the core of a young planet?"

Streaming lights against the canvas caught Stockwell's eye. While he'd been examining the blue and red diamonds, a new constellation had emerged onto the surface of the sphere and begun to glow.

A large yellow diamond appeared, then a tiny orange-ish, which circled the yellow. A pale green diamond was next, making a larger circle, then a blue, then a red, then larger diamonds of amber, chartreuse, and sky blue, until there were eight. Carl turned the lantern's flame down. Against the tent, the lights circled the pulsing yellow diamond at various speeds.

Stockwell looked to Carl, and then back to the canvas. "That can only be—"

Carl nodded, smiling. "Us. Our solar system."

Stockwell's voice was raspy. "The third light." He took a sip of rye. "That beautiful blue diamond. Earth."

"Incredible," said Carl, staring.

"And it's doing this every night?"

Carl nodded. "And if it's consistent with the past two nights, watch *this!*"

The solar system diamonds went dark, and chittered onto the crate, which now had a respectable pile—a fortune in discarded diamonds.

The solar system stones were replaced by many small crystals that Stockwell watched emerge from the liquid surface of the orb like ancient aliens clawing themselves free from a grave.

As before, the crystals were coal-dark until suddenly lighting up into brilliant orange, red, and yellow stars.

The new diamonds began to move and soon were silently racing over the glassy surface of the sphere and projecting streaks of yellow, orange, and red fire that streamed diagonally down the sheets of soiled canvas.

Stockwell was mystified. "What do you think this means? Is it trying to tell us something?"

"Not sure." Carl had his hand on his chin. "What does it look like to you?"

Stockwell answered without thinking. "Meteor shower."

Carl nodded, choked, as though he couldn't breathe in his excitement. "I think that this little orb is warning—signaling—an upcoming massive shower of some sort of cosmic debris. Perhaps we'll be passing through a broken-up comet we haven't mapped yet."

"The Younger Dryas Impact Hypothesis!" Stockwell bolted up, knocking his chair over.

"Our theory . . ." Carl's voice choked again. "Would be vindicated."

Our theory?

Still watching the beautiful streaks and then moving his eyes to the diamonds silently circling the black orb, Stockwell felt his excitement drain away. He picked up his chair and sat. "Except if that's what this is, then it could mean another civilizational and ecological wipe-out. You and I would be vindicated, but the Earth would be wiped clean. Start anew. A new era. But without us."

Carl tapped his index finger against his cheek. "I agree. If our speculations are correct, then earth could indeed be facing another extinction event. Like the asteroid impact that wiped out the dinosaurs, or the Younger Dryas-like trail of comets that instantly melted the arctic ice cap, scrubbing off the face of the earth the mysterious advanced civilizations of 12,800 years ago."

Then it hit Stockwell. "Has this alien—?" He searched for the right words. "This . . . *warning buoy* given any time implications? Any clues as to when the cataclysm might happen? If we're right, that is, about it warning us of an upcoming rain of fire."

The streaking lights flickered out and the diamonds slid off and onto the crate.

"How the hell does it do that?" said Stockwell.

"Do what?"

"Produce these diamonds and use them to communicate?"

Carl relit the kerosene lamp. "Easy. It must be pulling carbon from the air, then use unbelievable amounts of pressure and heat and—voila." He waved his hand over the crate, now carpeted with a rainbow of perfectly cut diamonds shimmering in the lamplight.

Carl could be so dense. "I *know* how diamonds are created," Stockwell huffed as he poured a finger of rye into the cup. He had to slow down. But with the voltage of this world-changing moment, he was too excited to feel drunk. Here they were, two hours south of Dallas, in the middle of a pasture in the black, moonless night, and he and Carl were the only two people on the *planet* who knew about this alien artifact.

Stockwell scooped up a handful of glittering stones. "You know what this means, don't you?" He ran his finger through what had to be hundreds of thousands, if not millions of dollars in perfect diamonds.

The surface of the orb trembled. And then ripples appeared, as though raindrops were falling into a black pool. New dark crystals emerged.

"This one is the strangest," said Carl, turning down the lamplight. "I have no clue."

"What is it?"

"Watch."

The diamonds moved and coalesced into strange patterns on the orb and then, as before, began to glow.

Stockwell rose. "Holy fuck. That's no constellation. It's a—"

"A figure." Carl interrupted. "My thoughts exactly."

"I can't fuckin' believe this."

A winged human-like body with an eagle's head sparkled onto the canvas. It was an Egyptian-style relief—torso facing forward with head and feet pointing to its right. One arm was extended awkwardly across its body clutching . . . Stockwell reached out to trace it on the canvas. "Is that a handbag?" The satchel dazzled intensely with all colors.

Carl's voice was low, but shaky. "Tom, I think we have stumbled onto the mystery of the gods who appeared all over the world, from Babylon to Turkey to New Zealand . . ."

"To Central America," Stockwell added. This was so great. They were riffing with one another, working to figure things out just like in the old days, when Stockwell was Carl's grad student. Before things went sour.

Carl looked to be in a trance. "The ancient, mysterious beings who resuscitated civilization after the wipeout 12,800 years ago. Permanently memorialized in stone monuments all over the world. Representing god-like messengers sent from the heavens. All carrying that mysterious bag."

"We never figured out what that bag represented," said Stockwell. "Or what it symbolized, or carried."

"No," said Carl, "and we still don't know. But it's beautiful, isn't it?"

The creature's wings glittered blue-silver, while the figure was a deep bronze, almost red. A heavy beard obscured the lower half of the thick-featured face. The bag dazzled like a rainbow made of stars.

"He looks like a god," said Stockwell.

"How else," Carl said, "could the ancients have interpreted creatures like this? Giants with magical powers."

"Carrying a bag of tricks."

"Indeed," said Carl.

The image faded and, in the resulting darkness, the diamonds slid off the orb in a now familiar clatter.

"If it repeats from the past two nights, this next will be the artifact's last message."

Next, it projected a stately procession of glyphs and symbols.

"Its language?" Stockwell mused.

"Has to be," said Carl. "Remember Voyager 2?"

Stockwell nodded as the alien glyphs marched across the canvas. "Launched in the 1970s. Carrying a plaque with symbols representing earth, images of a naked man and woman. Even an LP record made of gold, along with a stylus to play it so an alien civilization could hear sounds from earth."

"A probe to explore the outer planets," said Carl. "Turned into a buoy once it left the solar system, speeding through the oceans of space between stars."

Stockwell felt the thrill of a hunter who'd finally bagged his prey. "*This* is a buoy, Carl. Sent here to warn us."

As if Carl had flipped a switch, the glyphs faded away and the diamonds slid off the black ball and joined the pile on the crate.

Carl brightened the lamp. "I agree with you. I think we're onto something that will shake the earth, but we've got to have proof—not wild speculation."

Stockwell decided to take the initiative. "Let's put it in the back of my truck and take it to your lab." His voice caught in his throat. His truck. The truck he might not have tomorrow. How humiliating. An alien thing had landed in Carl's pasture and communicated something that was *actually* earth-shattering, and Stockwell was dreading the upcoming repo. Then he'd not even be able to *get* to Carl's lab to unravel the greatest cosmic mystery of the age.

But the solution to the truck issue was simple—money. And not a lot. "Well, one small benefit is that while you and I figure out the story behind this alien . . . *thing*, we can offload a diamond or two." He tried to sound light-hearted. "And solve a short-term fiscal difficulty I've found myself in."

"*Think*, Stockwell," said Carl dismissively, "this thing creates diamonds like us raking up gravel from a riverbed. DeBeers and industrial diamond manufacturers will be toast in a few years. The wealth isn't those trinkets on the crate. The wealth is in what we can learn!"

Stockwell's stomach was in his throat. All well and good, but these diamonds were a short-term answer to his problems. He kept his voice low. Calm-sounding, even. "Let's be smart about this, Carl. While we're figuring this out, we can skim a few. It wouldn't be a crime."

Carl shook his head emphatically. "If it got out that we delayed our investigation while selling these baubles, we'll be roasted in scientific circles and condemned by faculties from Austin to Cairo to Beijing. They'll call us fraudsters."

Stockwell was incredulous. "We'll still be studying the artifact. Who better than the two of us? We came up with the theory. This is our vindication!"

"You take too many shortcuts, Tom Stockwell. Science must be a methodical exploration from which reproducible theories are presented so colleagues can test our findings."

How to make Carl understand. "It's *not* a shortcut. Think of selling a few as a way to *fund* our research."

"That's what I mean," said Carl in his condescending father-correcting-his-six-year-old-son voice. "You're always looking for the easy path. There are no shortcuts in real science. It's slaving away until you have a theory you can present and defend."

Stockwell sighed. "You're misrepresenting what I'm saying. Think of all the receptions—all the boring cocktail parties you've spent securing funding. It's beneath us. The diamonds—"

"Baubles. The glory is in understanding what this little probe is trying to tell us—and then to prove it. We'll be *titans* of the academic world and we may even be able to help save civilization on earth."

Stockwell stared into the now-empty bottle of rye.

Carl sat down and his tone was conciliatory. "Tom, you and I—we live for *discovery*, not trinkets. Let's map out how we're going to study this. Get it into a lab. Interrogate it systematically. Heaven knows what secrets are locked up inside it. If it's a machine? Or alive? It may have answers to so many things. Unlimited clean power. We already know it can pull carbon from the air and store it in diamond form. That's worth a fuck of a lot more that selling the diamonds. *That's* where we need to focus."

Stockwell was defeated. "I get it. Can you let me take a couple? Half a dozen, if that? No one would know. And I've got these . . . *short-term* needs. It won't change anything about our study of the object."

Carl stood. "And when we go public with an announcement that will quake the world, you expect me to say, 'But at the beginning, I delayed my research by giving a bunch of diamonds to my former grad student so he could pay his *rent?*'"

The emphasis on *rent* cut deep.

Carl said, "I think you need to leave now. You'll have a better perspective in the morning. And we'll both be sober."

I could lose my truck tomorrow.

Stockwell's mind was going a thousand miles an hour. Everything was slipping away. *I have no income. And unlike Carl, I don't have the time to be patient.* Why couldn't Carl see things clearly? It wasn't a shortcut to take a few months to quietly sell some diamonds all over the world.

Maybe Carl wasn't the right person to solve this anyhow. *I'm the one who came up with the prototype of the theory. And I was right!* Stockwell felt the blood pounding in his temples. Perhaps he—Tom Stockwell—was the man for this job. The guy who could be the hero and solve the mysteries presented by the orb. And making a little on the side wouldn't hurt anything. Carl was so successful with his tenure and best-selling books that he was no longer tethered to the mortal world. The world of bills and payments and being short on cash at the end of the month. The things regular people had to do to get by. Life is about trade-offs. And Carl couldn't see that.

Carl picked up the shovel. "I'm going to bury this in the trench. I don't want to move it to the lab until I've got terms set with the administration so they can't take it away from me."

"*Think*, Carl. Whatever this sphere is, it was created by a wildly advanced and powerful intelligence."

Carl drove the shovel into the dirt. "Yes, yes."

"You tell *anyone*, I mean anyone, and they *will* take it from you. Your involvement will be *over*. You're naive if you think they'll let you run the studies. The whole project will be seized by the feds and you won't be allowed within a mile of it."

Carl tossed a shovel full of dirt. "Maybe. But that's the way I'm doing things."

Carl didn't have to dig much; the trench was already almost three feet deep. Dropping the shovel, he carefully picked up the black ball and kneeled, placing it gently into the temporary grave, caressing it.

What a spectacle! Carl was staring into the shining at the black ball like a lover.

Stockwell seethed. So selfish.

Stockwell's breaths were shallow and fast. He couldn't get enough air. He was suffocating. Carl was everything that was wrong with successful academics—no, everything wrong with successful *people*. They got into their castles and then pulled up the drawbridge. No empathy for those still clawing for a shard of success. Stockwell put his hands to his temples, trying to calm the galloping in his brain.

There was only one answer. As though watching himself in a movie, Stockwell staggered slightly as he rose. Carl was still kneeling, gently stroking the orb.

Stockwell tightened inside. On the dirt behind Carl.

The shovel.

He gripped the rough wood, raised it, and then held his breath. He slammed the rounded side into the back of Carl's head, where it connected with a sickening crunch.

Blood spattered the canvas and stung Stockwell's eyes.

Carl convulsed and then stiffened. Stockwell raised the shovel. But Carl lurched over into the trench, motionless.

Stockwell couldn't see well. He wiped at his eyes and the back of his hand was crimson and sticky.

Stockwell leaned over the newly-occupied grave. Carl's skull was shattered.

He felt calmer. The galloping had receded. Everything seemed suddenly clear.

He reached into the grave and gently lifted the orb and placed it on the crate. He then arranged Carl, turning him face up so he didn't have to look at the splintered back of his skull.

The blood on the orb! Turning to the crate, Stockwell watched the red drops slide off and pool on the wood.

He aimed the first shovelful of dirt at Carl's face. The still-opened eyes gave him the creeps.

Once Carl was buried, he'd strike the tent, take it home, and toss it onto his burn pile.

The right man to solve this mystery had stepped up and taken the reins.

And if something bad was heading for Earth, Stockwell would lead the efforts to design and build an underground city like Derinkuyu. Whatever humankind did to survive would be successful with Stockwell at the helm. He couldn't spend years bickering with Carl over every step. They might have only months. Or even days.

Patting down the grave with the shovel raised a cloud of dust. Stockwell looked to the empty bottle and swallowed, trying to clear his mouth and throat with his dirty spit.

He carefully scraped the diamonds from the crate and pocketed them.

Tapping his bulging pocket, he resolved to be better. The awesome responsibility of discovering what the alien thing was attempting to tell humanity was now on *his* shoulders. His alone.

A yellow star appeared on the orb. Then another—blue. The blue began to slowly circle the yellow. Once. Twice. Three times.

He needed to get busy. Dawn was only an hour or so away and he had a freakin' ton of work to do clearing the site.

As he carried the precious orb to his truck, he mused that Carl hadn't seen *this* signal—at least he hadn't talked about it. The blue diamond-star continued to orbit the yellow, creating enough light in the dark that Stockwell could see his way through unhooking the make-shift gate in the barbed wire fence. Suddenly feeling *very* drunk, he stumbled, almost dropping the ball. It wouldn't matter, he assured himself. The thing had traveled millions—billions—of miles through space and then survived a fiery descent through the atmosphere. It was indestructible.

After carefully placing the alien probe—what else could it be, really? —on the passenger seat he mused at the blue star circling the yellow, over and over. Another clue he'd have to figure out. But without Carl's help, unfortunately.

He looked to the East. No glow. He sighed. He felt so calm. At peace. Tomorrow he'd start over, fresh and new, once he'd burned the blood-spattered evidence.

The yellow star and its circling blue companion projected onto the roof of the truck's cab. How many times had it gone around?

He'd have to sit down and count it tomorrow night.

To hide the projected yellow and blue lights, Stockwell pulled the jacket draped over the back of the seat and covered the orb. "No time now, my friend. We'll talk tomorrow."

After he'd struck the tent and loaded the rest of Carl's shit into the bed of the truck, he raked and leveled the site.

As he was moving a few rocks onto the fresh grave, a rosy finger of dawn stabbed skyward in the East.

Time was on his side now. The time to do the investigation right. Just after he'd figured out how to globally launder millions of dollars in diamonds. He'd have to fly to places like Kazakhstan, Amsterdam, Moscow, and the diamond district in midtown Manhattan. All places where few questions would be asked.

Stockwell tossed the shovel into the bed of his truck and marveled at the vaporous peach, salmon, and coral that bled into the sky. He removed his hat and solemnly put it on his chest. *Today is the first day of my new life.*

Flashing red lights behind him jerked him from his reverie. Cops?

He turned. It was inside the cab. Opening the door he saw his jacket glowing like lava as tendrils of smoke rose lazily. *I need to show this to Carl.* Then he caught himself.

A red-rimmed hole grew in the back of his jacket. The stench of burning plastic and leather hit him so hard that he slammed the door and backed away as flames licked up and spread against the roof of the sealed cab.

Lost Souls

Kate Jonuska

SNEAKING OUT OF the house at midnight was easier than Robin expected. Every book and TV show had indicated kids needed trees or bedsheets to escape their bedrooms late at night, but her parents had reliably gone to bed at 10 p.m. Passing her brother's empty nursery, she simply used the front door, locking it behind her to walk casually into the suburban night. Unnecessary due to the full moon, Robin's pink mini flashlight swung from her backpack as she strolled along the empty streets of her neighborhood, all named after types of local cacti. Though she was barely double digits—recently 10 years old—Robin felt like the owner of the sleeping world as she walked the familiar route toward Paradise Memorial Gardens, the neighborhood cemetery and the site for tonight's mission.

Robin wasn't especially worried about getting into trouble for her graveyard outing. After all the trouble she'd gotten into lately, she'd already reached the worst level of punishment according to the hushed discussion in the kitchen she'd overheard the other night when she was supposed to be brushing her teeth.

"Now she's taken my eyeliners," her mom had said, obviously angry, "but I have no idea what to do about it. This obsession, it started as educational, and I know kids go through phases, but . . ."

Her father's voice was lower, carrying sound more than words as he replied, and Robin sensed a hollowness in his normal tone of assurance and warmth.

And in fact, for a while now, her family echoed hollow in ways Robin couldn't explain, their togetherness broken by the empty bedroom upstairs. Painted green with a border of cartoon jungle animals along the ceiling, the room felt threateningly empty, kind of like the emptiness of a black hole, full of heavy gravity and nothingness. But also not like that. For a while, during her third grade science unit on space, Robin had thought black holes were the coolest thing ever.

From her listening post on the stairs, though, she knew the educational obsession her parents were talking about was ancient Egypt, which was the subject of her fourth grade's history unit in the spring and had lodged firmly in her heart and mind ever since. At first, Robin's parents had tried relating to her. They'd handled her request for a short bob and straight bangs "like Cleopatra"—though the eyeliner as kohl had been new that night at dinner. They'd put up with her replacing her favorite stuffed animal to hug with a copy of the Book of the Dead under her pillow at night. Not that she'd been sleeping well with the black hole-like emptiness on the other side of her bedroom wall.

Robin's parents had become increasingly less cool since. She dug up a bunch of Iris bulbs and severed a sprinkler line when building a model pyramid burial in the backyard. The bulbs had sentimental value, her mom told Robin while perched on the girl's bed to explain, adding that gardening wasn't a bad thing, if she had permission and supervision. Her parents had given out two weeks of grounding with no screen time.

That punishment was then extended when Robin destroyed her collection of Barbie dolls by poking multiple holes with a crochet hook through their plastic bodies. She'd been practicing drawing out the dolls' brains and other organs with Egyptian mummification rituals using that favorite Book of the Dead. The full-color, illustrated copy from the museum gift shop told the story of the soul's journey after death and how to prepare the deceased for it. She could still remember buying the book on a family outing last year: a parent behind each of her shoulders, beaming down at Robin's interest and then smiling at one another. A warm and happy whole, back when her brother was still in Mom's stomach.

"You need to learn to take care of your possessions," her dad had said about the dolls when they'd added a month to her grounding.

"Also, no sleepovers or birthday parties in that time," Mom said, searching Robin's eyes for understanding. Not that Robin had been invited to many of those over the last year, ever since Robin had turned, as her friends said, "creepy AF."

Then for her next and biggest trouble so far, Robin had been sent to the principal's office for a meeting with her parents when she'd supposedly "threatened one of her classmates." In reality, Robin had told a friend that she should die when Robin did so they could be buried together and therefore spend their afterlife together in the endless field of reeds, the ancient Egyptian version of heaven. Robin had meant it as a compliment, not a threat, but obviously the girl was no real friend if she'd tattled.

The principal had decided against suspension, but that Big Trouble led to several visits to a child and family psychologist. In the doctor's office, Robin built pyramids out of plastic blocks and jabbered on to the doc about the Egyptian gods; Cleopatra and the Romans; mummification; tomb traps; and how the field of reeds was a heavenly place where all that was lost was recovered. Since those appointments had started, all of Robin's transgressions had produced only a thickening of the concern with which every adult treated her rather than any further discipline.

Her dad's voice was intelligible from the kitchen that night, before Robin heard him say, "The therapist says to take it slow. She'll find her way through this, with our help."

From the top of the stairs, Robin had an idea. *Finding the way.* Sometimes a soul did need help finding the way, which was why the Book of the Dead existed. With a determined nod of her bobbed hair, she planted the idea in her young heart like a seed, where it germinated and grew into a master plan that would somehow explain her obsession, heal her family, and mend the emptiness of a not-quite black hole. A promising, perfect plan.

Two nights later, she slung on her backpack full of tools and set off into the night. The route to the Paradise Memorial Gardens was familiar. Before their dog Casper had died—on the same date on which her brother was supposed to be born, which was called "irony"—her family often went to the cemetery. They'd walk their little mutt in the grassy graveyard among the headstones, burial plaques, and statues. When she asked why her dad didn't let Casper pee too close to the stones, he'd told her the park was "solemn," a place that invites us to think about the people buried in the earth while enjoying the great outdoors.

In this suburb of Phoenix, the great outdoors was often sweltering, its flora prickly, but the cemetery's solemnity had nonetheless imprinted upon Robin. Under the full moon, she steered clear of the mausoleum at the south end of the cemetery, a big, marble-tiled building that she loved but that was only open during the day. She'd spotted at least one camera when she cased the joint yesterday. Instead, she plodded toward the artificial pond in the middle of the gardens. The kidney-shaped water feature was framed with a concrete border, and a fountain sprayed eight feet in the air in the center, always on despite the desert and her dad's grumbling about "short-sighted water policy." The pond's swans were asleep, but the fountain gurgled like the fertile and life-giving River Nile.

Under the city-dimmed stars, Robin listened and thought she understood what her dad meant in calling the place solemn. Her senses were heightened by her rebellion, and she could hear her breath in her skull, feel her knees squishing into the watered grass as she knelt.

Solemn meant she wasn't just taking a walk. She was on a quest, and like any heroine on a quest, she had a higher purpose: her brother, the one who had been lost. At first, Robin hadn't understood the adult definition of a lost baby, meaning a medical event that ended the pregnancy. For her, the miscarriage had been ominous and inconceivable, and despite all the explanations, it still seemed to Robin that her brother had evaporated into thin air. At the hospital, her mom had cried and screamed for her baby, then the adults debated about how old a baby needed to be to be called a baby. Robin had never seen his body. His ashes were now in a tiny box, and according to her parents, he'd skipped the bodily world to go straight to the spiritual one.

As the expert in the realm of death, however, Robin knew that was totally not how it worked. Every soul needed to undertake a journey to reach the field of reeds, a.k.a. heaven. Obviously, this had not been a journey her brother had been able to undertake, meaning his soul was instead lost, had been denied the afterlife, and was being erased into non-existence. Nothing, just total sucking emptiness, like his bedroom felt. So in order to fix her family, Robin obviously would have to complete the journey of her brother's soul on his behalf.

Luckily, she knew exactly how. For a soul's journey to be successful, Anubis, the jackal-headed god of mummification and guide through the afterlife, needed to determine a soul's worthiness by weighing the heart against a feather, each placed on one side of a scale. Opening a folder from her backpack, she placed an 18-inch-long peacock feather she'd found at the zoo on the grass beside her.

As for the other side of the scale, her brother's heart hadn't beaten on its own, had been lost with the rest of that body, leaving nothing to weigh. But she'd thought of that. Robin next placed a handmade doll on the grass, a crocheted figure of a smiling little boy made by her grandma and which had been living in the black hole of the nursery until Robin liberated it. Despite knowing she should take good care of possessions, she'd opened one of the seams to insert a small amount of her brother's ashes, which she'd stolen from the fireplace mantle and kept in a sandwich bag. Once sewn back up with uneven stitches, she'd shaken the ashes into the stuffing, readying the doll for mummification.

The rest of her kit included her full-color coffee table version of the Book of the Dead spread to the pertinent pages; a kitchen scale; her embalming/sewing tools; and the small, lidded canonic jars she'd made at an after-school pottery class. The teacher had assumed the tiny containers were for playing kitchen rather than for organs, and Robin had let him assume. Under the light of the full moon and with occasional help from her flashlight, Robin used her tools and her Barbie-practiced skills to very carefully embalm her lost baby brother. She hooked stuffing mixed with ashes through the fabric of the doll and placed each organ-shaped wad into the correct organ jar.

Deep inside her brain, Robin was frightened she might just be playing pretend, but her actions and their repetition had come to feel—that word again—solemn. After all, so much of science seemed like magic from far away, and so much of the adult world seemed to work on symbols. Like her parents' wedding rings were symbols of their love but didn't actually keep them together, like magnets. The rings still worked, though; her parents said so. Her symbolic brother could have power, too, could also be the real kind of magic.

As the fountain/River Nile gurgled, Robin worked. The kitchen scale hadn't been a great choice, she discovered, since she could only weigh one item at a time. She was forced to weigh the feather and faux heart separately, each of them very light, while the stakes were very heavy. This quest was literally about life and death. Her hand shook, the stupid scale was hard to see, and just when Robin began to think her entire quest was going to fall apart, she sensed the heat of eyes upon her.

Silhouetted against the sky, a large dog that probably weighed as much as Robin herself, a big fourth grader, sat not three feet away in the opposite direction of home. His wide chest tapered toward his legs, the front two held together primly and the back two tucked beneath an upright, skinny tail. Its large, squarish head made Robin assume the dog male, and she thought him maybe a Doberman and greyhound mix? But solid black, without a Doberman's chocolate spots. Most importantly, the dog's ears were tall and upright, curved near the end.

"Anubis," Robin whispered, recognizing the god's famous face. The dog-headed god must have taken his fully canine form. Her eyes widened in the moonlight to their stretching limits.

The dog was striking, the kind of animal she would have taken note of on an owner's leash around the neighborhood—though maybe new, unnoticed dogs had arrived since Casper passed away. Still, he had no collar, no sign of ownership, but his short coat was glossy and clean. The dog turned his head to meet Robin's stare, and her chest froze in fear at his red eyes.

But Anubis's gaze only rested upon her for a moment, then slid away back toward the grass and Robin's work. When she looked back at what she'd created, Robin was struck by how ominous the scene looked, moonlight glinting on the crochet hook like a weapon.

The dog sniffed. Once, twice. His nostrils alone moved. He looked to Robin once more, and their eyes met, about the same distance off the ground. The dog then took one step, two, toward the symbol of Robin's baby brother. He sniffed each of the jars, lingered over the kitchen scale, smelled the feather, the doll, the scale again. The whites (and reds) of his eyes flashed at Robin once more, the dog moving slowly and methodically while Robin held her breath.

He bowed, sitting onto his haunches and stretching out his paws directly toward the brother doll. Robin had seen dogs bow to play, but this dog was so… solemn and sure and slow. Until he wasn't. In the blink of an eye, Anubis grabbed up Robin's brother in his mouth and took off like a greyhound shot. Over several lanes of pavement across the street, he disappeared into an open lot of dust and desert grasses soon to be more homes—"and more wasteful water fountains, no doubt," according to Dad. That lot could totally be the Arizona entrance to the endless field of reeds, at least symbolically. After all, Robin even had the symbolic Nile at her back. Magic could be real.

After a moment of stillness, Robin's breathing returned to normal, but her heart was lighter than usual, perhaps lighter than a feather, as she gathered up the Book of the Dead and her tools into her backpack. Her parents' bedroom door was still closed and dark when she silently unlocked and relocked the front door and crept upstairs. She passed her brother's room, now just a room, quiet and still in the night. Everyone was safe and found. In her bed, the kohl/eyeliner she forgot she'd drawn around her eyes for the ritual smudged into her pillow as Robin got the best night's sleep she'd had since third grade.

Out of Context

Laura Blegen

FOR CENTURIES, THE Kingdom of Ritathe had benefited from the prominence it gave its Scholars, and the technological and cultural advantages those Scholars provided in return. Some long-ago Queen had built a Nautilus-shaped building for them, its hall spiraling inward, and the University had grown up around it. Due to his long dedication to Inerin, the God of Wisdom, Scholar Wilistan had earned an office that was near the center of the highest winding curve, fully three floors above the outer ring. There were stairwells and other passages that cut across, for those who knew the building's secrets, but visitors never made it that far without a guide, and no one knocked on his door by mistake.

When a knock did come, late one night, it jolted his attention away from the document he'd been studying: a few pages from ten-year-old letter that he'd found earlier in the day, buried in a box that had been shoved into a corner for years. He'd only gotten to it now because Provost Ameias's special inquiry had forced a change in his priorities. He hadn't expected to find something like this, with potentially profound impacts for the country. He glanced at the clock: it was after midnight. Generally, he liked working late. Without interruptions, he could sink so deeply into his work that the rest of the world disappeared entirely.

But tonight, the provost's insistent pleas were driving everyone out of their usual routines. There were probably a dozen Scholars, maybe more, still at their desks, combing through piles of documents to satisfy a single patron with political motivations. Provost Ameias herself might still be prowling the halls, trying to motivate results by interrupting their work, he thought with a resentful grumble. He covered the letter on his desk with the book closest to hand.

The knock came again, but it was diffident, and barely loud enough to be heard. Definitely not Provost Ameias. He relaxed slightly and replaced the solar stone in the mage-crafted illuminator on his desk. Immediately, the shadows at the corners of his office receded.

"Enter," he called.

The thick wooden door swung open to reveal an eight-year-old girl bending to pick up the load of short archival boxes she'd briefly set on the floor outside. She straightened and flashed a weak smile as she brought the pile through the door.

"Banyan," he said, "It's awfully late for you to be working, isn't it?"

"I guess it is a little bit, sir," she replied, hesitating just inside the doorway. Realizing he didn't have any empty surfaces for her to put her burden on, Wilistan turned in his chair, ignored a twinge in his back, and carefully lifted some papers off a decoratively carved side table. Banyan set the boxes down there. "Provost Ameias has the archivists working extra this nine-day, so they asked us to stay, too."

Wilistan struggled not to show his concern. Bad enough that Ameias had commandeered the attention of every Scholar with expertise even remotely related to her special inquiry, but the archivists were technically independent of the Scholars' Nautilus. They served the whole university, and the city beyond it. He couldn't imagine any justification for this kind of injunction.

"Can I ask, sir? What is it you are looking for? They've had us carrying boxes of materials all over the campus for three days, but I never get to see what's in them."

"You know what's in them, Banyan. Old records, letters, journals. Mostly very boring things."

"Not boring at all though, sir! The best stories come from old documents, right?"

"Of course," he said. Despite the hour, he found himself warming to a lecture he usually gave to students two or three years older than the girl before him. Increasingly, his introductory course on research had become the only thing he found worth pausing his studies for an hour or two. "Any box in the archives *might* have a great revelation in them, but most do not. We keep them because we don't yet know what will be important in the future."

"And you need to look at them now because whoever packed them away didn't know what would be important today."

This wasn't the first time that his casual conversations with the page revealed a quick thinker. "Exactly. That's why the archives are so valuable. They contain the entire history of Ritathe, each event recorded from dozens of different perspectives and stowed safely away in the form of private letters and trade records." Most of it made for pretty dry reading, he thought, but he didn't want to dim her enthusiasm too much.

"So, what is important now?" the girl said, her hand lingering on the lid of one of the boxes she'd carried in for him. "Maybe I could help. This was my last errand of the day, and if you tell me what you're looking for, I could look, too. I'm the best reader in my Temple class."

Wilistan struggled to contain a chuckle for fear of hurting her feelings. It was delightful to see such interest in a child.

"Reading is just the beginning," he said. "We're not looking for specific words, but the meanings behind them, perhaps even the meanings behind those. Things left unsaid."

Her head tilted to one side. “How can you search for something people *didn’t* say?”

“That’s a good question. You have to know a lot about the topic, to start with. Since the provost is looking for information about Ritathe’s neighbor, the country of Gasteng, I imagine you’ll find all the Scholars in Gastengor history and language in their offices tonight.” Wilistan realized that he’d subconsciously put one hand on the book that covered the document he’d been reading when he saw Banyan’s eyes fall there. He deliberately folded his arms over his chest before he continued. “That’s not my expertise, but as a Scholar in church history, I know a lot about the conflicts between our religion and theirs. These boxes contain the writings—both personal and public—of people that have engaged in that debate or converted from one religion to the other.”

“They don’t follow the Triad?” Banyan asked, her head tilted slightly as if she couldn’t imagine such a thing.

“No, they worship a single god. There are some Scholars who argue that their one god has aspects of each of the Triad—Cadais’s leadership, Inerin’s wisdom, and Ahelia’s stewardship of life and death—but the church in Gasteng rejects that. Their forms of worship are quite different from ours, as well.” Wilistan had to stop himself from launching into another lecture.

“Is that what the provost wants to know? Will their church be a problem in the prince’s negotiations?”

Wilistan frowned. There was no reason for an eight-year-old to concern herself with the negotiations between Ritathe and Gasteng. He wanted to model the process of scholarly research at its best, and not this form, corrupted by people with political motivations. “It hasn’t been a problem before. Our two countries have been working around our differences for years. What the provost is looking for now is more complicated. We might not know what we’re looking for until we find it.”

“That sounds hard,” Banyan said, her face scrunching in imagined discomfort.

“It can be sometimes,” he said, “But the work I’m describing is still many years in your future, if you decide this is the path you want. You’ll get plenty of training to be successful. The pursuit of wisdom can be very rewarding, when you immerse yourself in learning enough to feel the hand of Inerin guiding you.”

He might have kept going, but he saw the girl’s body sway with fatigue.

“For now, though, you only need focus on the tasks directly in front of you. It’s very late. If that was your last delivery of the day, you should get some sleep. Do you have a safe way home?”

“I can walk, sir. It’s alright.”

Wilistan frowned. From what he knew of Banyan’s background, her walk home crossed half the city. This time of night, that would put her through at least a couple of neighborhoods where unsavory types might be watching for a vulnerable child like her. She wasn't the only one, either. Given university hierarchies, none of the kids stuck on the late shift lived in the comfortable neighborhoods closer to campus. Provost Ameias had no idea that her fool search had collateral effects like this.

"No, it certainly is not alright. Gather up any other pages that are finishing their work for the night and go to the stable. Tell them that Scholar Wilistan wants you all to get home safely, by carriage." He reached into a desk drawer for a scrap of paper and quickly wrote out a note authorizing the expense.

Despite her brave words, she didn't hesitate to snatch the paper from his fingers. "Thank you, sir," she said, and carefully let herself back out into the hall. "Goodnight!" she called, as she closed the door behind her.

"Goodnight, little one," he said quietly to the closed door. At her age, he'd have given anything to live in the city, away from the sons of hunters and lumberjacks that had tortured the skinny, bookish boy in their midst. He'd only later realized that children faced dangers everywhere, when adults didn't look after them properly.

Wilistan pushed those thoughts away and turned his attention back to his desk, uncovering the letter. He read it again, carefully checking his translation from the original Gastengor because there were a few idioms he wasn't accustomed to. His interpretation held steady. Despite what he'd said to Banyan, this document said exactly what it meant. The writer's animosity toward Ritathe and its religion was right on the surface, along with the beginnings of a plot to weaken the Ritathan government. Banyan herself could have identified this letter as relevant to the provost's search, but Banyan wasn't old enough to understand the damage that incomplete knowledge could do.

In his class, Wilistan taught students the difference between information and understanding. This letter was only one perspective, one person's opinion. His students quickly learned to start their examination of sources with two basic questions:

Who wrote it? That was a mystery, unfortunately, since the final page was missing. Even the prince would want that answer, sooner or later. The negotiations would pause, either way, but whether they ever continued might depend on whether this inflammatory document had been written by someone in close contact with the Gastengor royal family, or by an isolated dissident.

It was the second question that caused Wilistan's hesitation tonight. *Who was the audience, and what do we know of their opinion on the subject?*

Wilistan had found the letter among the not-yet-archived personal effects of the late Lord Roger det'Falsonne, born and raised in Gasteng. He'd moved to Ritathe as a young man and, within a few years, had married into the family of one of the

King's closest advisors. He had gone through a very public conversion to the Ritathan religion and kept a series of journals about his changing beliefs. Those journals were the reason his widow had brought his things to Wilistan first, before they were archived. They'd been sitting on the floor of his office for a shameful period of time, but he still remembered the widow clearly, and her son, clinging to her skirts, with his mourning clothes looking stiff and awkward on his small form. The boy had been so small and vulnerable, but he'd be a year or two older than Banyan now. The same age Wilistan had been when he'd first arrived at the University, traveling by river barge with three broken ribs bound tightly, and all his hopes tied up in a single letter from his village cleric, which he'd clutched in one sweaty hand.

That letter had saved Wilistan, but the one on his desk might doom the Falsonne boy. Its author had clearly assumed a sympathetic listener in det'Falsonne. If that assumption was correct, Lord Roger had been a liar and a heretic, at best, and potentially an agent for a hostile enemy government. Whichever anti-Gasteng faction drove Ameias's inquiry would seize this partial-truth to make their point, and Roger det'Falsonne would be posthumously condemned, with no one to speak for him.

Perhaps Ameias would call for a deeper inquiry before she took the letter to her supporters. So far, Wilistan had found no explanation or even reference to the letter in det'Falsonne's journals. Further research might reveal whether the man had agreed with or abhorred the sentiments of his correspondent. If Ameias held back a few days, Scholars could either support a condemnation with actual evidence, or clear an innocent man's name.

Ameias was in a hurry, though. She might choose to perform the follow-up research after releasing the letter or skip it altogether. After all, Roger det'Falsonne was no longer alive to suffer the consequences.

His family, however, would suffer them in his stead. The vines of rumor grew faster than any serious inquiry could hope to forestall. There might not be official consequences for the family, but given current tensions, no one would want to be seen aligning themselves with potential traitors. His widow would find herself without allies or support. The boy would be cut off from any prospects they'd been developing for his future, and the target of whichever bullies had the run of this generation.

Wilistan ran his left hand over a scar on his neck, just under his ear. Roger det'Falsonne's survivors would soon discover that they'd be safer in exile than at court, all because of a letter that had been written before the boy was even born.

Wilistan held the boy's future in his hands, and he hated the feeling. He was a Scholar, not an Adjudicator. That distinction was exactly the point, though, he told himself as he reached for an empty protective folder and placed the letter inside. Scholars provided information. His vows and his duties were clear. Provost Ameias, in her wisdom, would take it from here.

He pushed his chair back from the desk and stood up. This wasn't his decision to make, but he felt the weight of it anyway. It made his body—already slow with age—struggle with the necessary forward movement. Each step felt like reminding his legs how to do what should have felt natural. Still, he took the long curving hall tonight, with no shortcuts. He couldn't bring himself to rush.

Beyond the university community, there were those who thought the shape of the Nautilus encouraged insularity and separation from the outside world. They weren't wrong, exactly, but they didn't understand the purpose behind it. Scholars weren't confined to the reclusive world of their studies. They never forgot they were part of a larger one that moved much faster than the work they did on the inside. But centuries of experience had shown that a Scholar's best work happened when they'd found some distance, both literal and figurative, from political pressures and the hectic pace of the city.

As Wilistan walked, he mentally repeated the vows he'd made decades ago. To Inerin and to the community of Scholars, he had pledged to relentlessly pursue truth. To share knowledge freely both inside and outside the Nautilus. To hold nothing back in his pursuit of wisdom, because wisdom could never be reached by jealously hoarding information.

The provost had an office in the outer-most hall of the building, and the only living apartments on campus outside the student dormitories. This theoretically kept her responsive to both Scholars and the larger community. In moments, Wilistan could hand over this responsibility to the person who'd asked for it. She'd be glad to hear from him, even this late.

That was the problem, though, he thought as he paused a dozen meters shy of the provost's door. Scholarly work shouldn't be rushed like this. He thought of Banyan, only eight years old and practically asleep on her feet and expected to walk home after dark. Ameias had ordered that without a second thought, just like the adults who'd looked the other way every time Wilistan's tormentors had him cornered somewhere. As a child, Wilistan hadn't thought to blame those adults for the injuries he'd suffered, but his perspective had shifted since then.

He'd never thought of Ameias as a bad person. He'd known her since they were both students—nearly forty-five years now. If they'd never really been friends, that was as much because of their differing interests as anything else. Ameias enjoyed lavish receptions and parties, while Wilistan preferred his social engagements to be quiet. He was happy to chat with tradespeople and the families of his students, but he abhorred the formality of court presentations and events, and preferred to avoid any commitments that might require his attendance there.

Ameias, on the other hand, thrived in the light of powerful people, so Wilistan had not hesitated to throw his support behind her when the previous provost had announced his retirement. He didn't want the job, preferring to focus on his own research without the pressures that came with a position of power. He longed to let her continue to face that onslaught of attention, and return to his solitude, even now. He could choose that. All he had to do was cross the remaining distance and knock on her door.

The sound of quiet voices pulled him out of his reverie. Three pages, Banyan among them, came up behind him, heading toward an exterior door to his right. Banyan was the youngest of the three; the other two had probably started taking classes on campus. All three looked worn out by their long hours.

"Thank you, Scholar," one of the boys said, with a half-hearted bow. Clearly, Banyan had told them who was sponsoring their carriage ride home.

"Say, do any of you know the Falsonne boy?" Wilistan asked. He gestured at the oldest. "He's about your age, I imagine."

When that boy nodded, Wilistan continued, "What can you tell me about him?"

"He's quiet, sir. Seems pretty sad all the time. Keeps to himself, which I think is because he's small, sir."

There was something else, Wilistan could see. Something that the boy wouldn't share with an adult he didn't know well. Wilistan could guess, though, from what he'd already heard. Lord Roger's son already had bullies targeting him, although they were probably being clever about it for now. Once they heard their parents badmouth his father, it would feel like tacit permission for brutality.

Wilistan waved the children away and watched them go out into the night. He hesitated before he followed them out. He needed a moment to think. The children had gone to the left, following the wide path connecting the Nautilus to the enormous building which contained all four of the university's libraries.

Wilistan went the other way, down a narrow stone path that meandered through a garden designed and cultivated for thoughtful strolls. It had thick hedges, berry brambles, and gnarled trees that quickly concealed its paths from the rest of campus, and even from one another. Wilistan followed the particular path which led to a small shrine to Inerin, practically hidden under the branches of a locust tree.

The Nautilus contained a grander temple, more modern, with rows of comfortable chairs. The beautiful paintings on its walls were meant to inspire Scholars and visitors alike with the beauty of enlightenment under the God of Wisdom. It was there that students were first taught the prayers of the dedicants, where each Scholar took their vows, and where they would eventually be mourned.

However, Wilistan's thoughts tonight had been repeatedly drawn back to his own childhood in a small town far from the capital. So often, he'd sought refuge in the woods and found himself begging comfort from the Triad there. Perhaps that's why he'd received his calling from Inerin under the light of His full moon. This simple monument brought him closer to that first pure experience than anything else.

The moon wasn't full tonight—that might have been too much to ask—but the sky was blessedly clear, so even a half-moon provided enough illumination to help him across the garden. He approached the shrine and settled himself carefully on a stone bench a few yards away. The moonlight filtering through tree branches was just enough to highlight the worn gray stone.

For a moment, he sat, breathing in the scents of damp earth and allowing his body to calm, his breath to slow, until he felt less like an intruder on the night, and more like a part of it. Then, he counted three slow breaths before he began his prayer.

"Most Wise Inerin, open my mind, make ready my heart, and guide my search."

He faltered. Already, the words of a lifetime of prayer were wrong. It was not the search that he needed help with. Indeed, the target of his search weighed down his robes more than a single piece of paper ought to. He inhaled once more and tried again, although he felt his voice shake with the truth.

"Wisdom, I need your help."

He hesitated again, looked around at the empty garden, and pulled out the folder.

"You taught our first Scholars that truth is found only in the consideration of many perspectives. I fear that the current political moment will drive people, both inside and outside the gates of this institution, to rash decisions without taking enough time for that consideration. A child will suffer the consequences if the information I hold is not handled well."

Wilistan let his voice trail off, unable to put words to his fears that Ameias could not be trusted to do so. Instead, he sat, as had been the habit of his youth, and watched the moonlight stretch and warp the shadows of the garden.

It had been too long, he realized, since he had done this. He'd gotten too accustomed to staying indoors at night, to only seeing the world under bright sunlight or the steady and predictable light of solar stones. He had forgotten how a thing could change its appearance entirely, depending on the angle of the light. How a shrub could conceal its shape and the treachery of its thorns in large, soft, shadows. How something larger, like a tree, could create the illusion of a man watching him from under its branches.

Suddenly, the shape under that tree was not just a shadow. It solidified in a way that was both very real and terrifyingly unearthly. Wilistan was certain that moments before, he had been alone in the garden, and now someone stood where no one could be.

His mouth dried, and he struggled to put sound to the words that crowded his mind. He had heard stories of Inerin's visitations. He'd even hoped for one when he was younger, the way all initiates secretly hope to be the exception, but he learned to look for Inerin's guidance in subtle ways. Every prayer he'd ever learned seemed inadequate now that the god himself stood so close.

"My Lord," he said, finally, trying not to stammer.

"Wilistan." The voice did not come from the figure in the shadows but from the air all around them. The silence that followed was thick and heavy, blocking out all the usual sounds of night. It stretched out, painfully, until Wilistan realized that Inerin, the god to whom he'd devoted his life, was waiting for him to speak.

"Forgive me, my Lord. Your presence is… unexpected."

The man-shaped shadow darkened and seemed to be leaning in his direction. Wilistan found himself instinctively leaning away from it.

"Why?" The single syllable echoed and probed at him from all directions.

Why, indeed? All three gods in the Triad had appeared to humans during the Founding. Since then, Cadais had kept his interactions brief and symbolic, and Ahelia had stayed blessedly removed, but the God of Wisdom had continued to bless his followers with dialogue. The histories contained hundreds of examples—Scholars on the verge of career-making discoveries guided in the last moments by a celestial hand—but the last of those had been years ago, and Wilistan hadn't heard of a single time that Inerin had appeared to someone hiding in a garden from something they didn't want to do.

"I am a humble Scholar, My Lord. There are much greater minds than mine, wrestling with bigger questions."

Wilistan counted five of his own heartbeats, before the voice echoed around him. "Many pray to Cadais instead, even when they say my name."

Wilistan wasn't sure what to make of that. Or how to ask his question. Now that he faced the god directly, it seemed dangerous to ask permission to disobey his oaths.

This might be his only audience with Inerin, his one chance in a lifetime of work, and something most Scholars would never experience. It was dizzying for a historian to suddenly realize the historic moment he occupied. His current concern—the future of one child—paled in comparison to a lifetime of questions about the nature of time and divinity.

Wilistan felt the air move around him in a series of small buffeting breezes and realized that his god had chuckled. Too late, he remembered that the God of Wisdom could read thoughts.

"Your mind cannot contain a greater understanding of either time or divinity, I'm afraid," said the voice. "So those will have to wait until you are no longer contained in this human form."

Wilistan grasped at that small hint. "Will I have consciousness then? To understand?"

"Of a sort," Inerin replied, but he sounded bored with the question. "I find it difficult to follow a single human life at its end."

Wilistan struggled not to wince at that dismissive response. Inerin was attracted to ideas, not to individuals. His disinterest in the mundanities of human life was well recorded, along with his consistent refusal to take a side in political concerns. On the other hand, the god was here, now. He had come in response to something in Wilistan's prayer.

“Does that mean this negotiation—or this boy—is particularly important?”

The air around him lost substance for a moment. When it returned, Wilistan had the intimate sense of what a cosmic shrug felt like.

“No, neither the boy nor these negotiations will impact anything of importance *to me.* I came merely to see you, the Scholar who prays in the old ways.”

Wilistan swallowed. There were Scholars who examined tiny parts of nature with pieces of magnifying glass, and he suddenly felt like one of those minuscule creatures with a god looking through at him.

“Does that mean you don’t have an answer for my question…?” he began.

“I have already answered you. The rest is for you to wrestle with. You don’t have long before the sunrise.”

Then He was gone. The thickness in the air dissipated like fog in a breeze, and Wilistan heard an owl calling in the distance, heralding the return of all the normal night sounds. He sat alone in the garden with no more certainty than he’d had before.

I have already answered you, the god had said. Wilistan turned their brief conversation over in his mind and came back to one disturbing thing. Prayers to Cadais in Inerin’s name. Cadais, the highest of the Triad. God of Power, represented by the sun. In older writings, they used a different turn of phrase, no longer popular. They'd referred to him then as God of Ambition.

Leaning into that old interpretation, one could hear, in Inerin's comment, a concern that others at the university were allowing ambition to overtake their pursuit of wisdom. Ambition had been what caught Inerin's attention, but He had appeared to Wilistan instead. Was that simply because of his old-fashioned ways, or was it because of the doubts he'd brought into his prayers? Wilistan shivered to think that Inerin had chosen him, instead of the person Wilistan was supposed to trust with this decision.

He slowly stood up from the bench, his knees aching in protest even as the backs of his thighs rejoiced that they were no longer pressing against cold stone. He turned toward the door, craving a fire to warm himself while he decided what to do.

Inerin's final words stopped him. *You don't have long before the sunrise.* That was literally true, but also figuratively. Not long before Ameias would seek him out to see what another day's research had gained them. If he believed she was blinded by ambition, he couldn't trust her with the letter he held.

Carefully, Wilistan put the letter in his pocket and turned in a slow circle. He looked around the garden as if he could find better options planted in its beds. If he put the letter back where he'd found it, where it arguably belonged, someone would find it. Probably soon, given current interests. With a sinking heart, he realized that he'd mentioned det'Falsonne's collection to one of the archivists the day before. He couldn't hold it back for long.

His eyes landed on a trowel leaning up against a small gardener's shed. For a moment, his imagination ran away with the romantic notion of literally burying the letter here in Inerin's shrine. It would be the safest option for the boy, letting the damp earth have its way with fragile paper and ink, but Wilistan couldn't bring himself to do it. Despite his concerns about the university's current leadership, destroying an original source document like this went against everything that made him who he was. Everything that had transformed him from a scared boy to a man with the power to protect someone else.

He eyed the stone path under his feet. He could follow it away from the building, as it curved back toward the campus gates. He ached for his bed, and he could stash the letter somewhere in his apartments, except for his nosy landlady. He'd never minded her before, since he rarely brought work home with him, but he was sure she'd find this among his things somehow.

Only his office remained. There were stacks in the corners that had been there for years and would probably remain until he died and someone cleared out his things. He'd just have to live until the boy was safely an adult with accomplishments and allies of his own. Wilistan snorted, bemused, as he hauled the door open to go back inside. He wasn't as old as all that, yet.

"Oh, Wilistan, it's you."

Surprise stopped him in his tracks. He turned to find Provost Ameias standing in the doorway of her office, one hand braced against the doorframe. She wore her academic robes, but her hair, usually carefully arranged, was pulled back under a sleep cap.

"Were you talking to someone? I thought I heard voices . . ."

"Just myself," he said. When her eyebrows narrowed, he added, "And Inerin, of course. I took a moment in the shrine to clear my head."

"Ah, that's an old country habit, isn't it? Praying outdoors?"

Something in her tone rankled him, even if he'd just been thinking the same thing.

"Perhaps," he countered, carefully. "But I find the cool air helps me see things differently."

He started to turn away, but then stopped again.

"Provost? The next luncheon for senior faculty is tomorrow, isn't it?"

She nodded slowly; her eyes watchful.

"I'll be there," he said, and tried not to react to the look of surprise that crossed her face. His dislike for such events was perhaps too well known. "Now, if you'll excuse me, I think we both had better get some sleep."

He nodded politely and turned toward his office. As the hall curved away from her, he thought about the lines in her face, the tension in the hand which had gripped her doorframe.

He didn't want her job any more than before. But perhaps he shouldn't lose himself so completely in his research going forward. He could go to more receptions and get to know the nobles who supported the University's work. Perhaps he could see what drove Ameias and the other academic leaders away from Inerin's guidance. Perhaps, if he applied himself to understanding this problem like any other, he could lead them back again.

Wilistan took a shortcut back upstairs, although his left knee crackled on every step. Back in his office, he considered his options. The bookshelf closest to his desk was bursting with materials he either used frequently himself or kept handy for discussions with students. On the opposite wall, the shelves were slightly less crowded. They contained some of his favorite books but also a few that he could quietly admit to himself lived there more for the appearance of legitimacy than for any usefulness. A leather-bound collection of every thesis published in the Nautilus's first three years collected dust on the top shelf. Every Scholar had that set, and no one ever opened them. Wilistan reached for one and placed the letter carefully inside.

When he'd returned the book to its place, he paused at his desk with a hand on the research notes that awaited his attention. He would miss the long, isolated hours devoted to nothing but this. He'd have to learn to be more efficient, perhaps take on an assistant, to free his time for other commitments. The Nautilus couldn't afford for him to stay too much inside.

Particulate

Jessica Lavé

CARL BLINKED AT his furry brown and white feet as he awoke groggy from his nap. His ears twitched at an unexpected rumble from somewhere else in the house. When the rumble shifted into a huge crash, he leapt so high he almost bonked his head on the ceiling of the den. The silverware rattled in the drawers and some of the plastic cups and boxes fell off the countertops. He turned to look for his mother and his siblings, but they had left the den, an empty cabinet underneath the kitchen sink. Left him alone. With the roaches. And the ants. And those nasty spiders that bit him when he slept.

He arched his back, then slid his front paws out in front of him to stretch the opposite way. He listened, flicking his ears at every noise the old, creaky house made, trying to discern the sounds of his family from the familiar squeaks and groans of the floors: a rustle against the stacks of magazines, a clickety scurry of the cockroaches against the hardwood floors between mountains of food waste and mail and trash, the rhythmic spinning of the ceiling fan that never turned off, the old man's rickety recliner—abandoned for at least a week now, and the television blaring out some cooking show. Through all that, he listened but heard no patter of cat paws, no purrs, mews, or growls.

Carl didn't know what that rumble and crash could have been. He hadn't made it very far outside the den yet—he was growing slower than his siblings, and the stairs were still too tall for him to climb; they might as well have been giant trees. But if the upstairs was anything like the downstairs, some heap of books, cookware, glass, or—most likely—garbage, had fallen from its shelf or perch or mound, and crashed down wherever there was room to land. He hoped his family hadn't been caught underneath whatever had crashed—his mama and siblings had started spending more time upstairs over the past couple weeks.

Carl knew to tread carefully, not to brush up too closely against anything. His legs were short, and he was very clumsy, but he had learned to watch his step. He had seen the mountains of junk collapse. Sometimes it was just empty, moldy pizza boxes, but sometimes the heaps of big trash bags held heavier things like dishes or shoes.

The worst day was when Georgia, the most curious of his siblings, had been playing with a cockroach, chasing and pouncing, racing and batting, until she slid too far across the little patch of hard floor and whacked into a stack of CDs. The CDs held up a pile of dirty laundry, and the laundry pile held a cardboard box full of books. The CDs went everywhere, and the laundry toppled sideways, but the books… the books slid off the top and fell right onto Georgia. Carl would never forget the sound she made, somewhere between a shriek of terror and a howl of pain, but worse, he would never be able to forget the crunch that the box of books made when it landed on her. It had been hard for a few weeks, with her right there and not being able to do anything about it, her body stinking and decomposing and not being able to avoid it. But eventually, the smell of death faded enough that Carl and the others didn't notice it so much anymore, and the day-to-day work of keeping six kittens alive was enough to keep Mama preoccupied so she didn't think about Georgia too much.

That crash upstairs, and not seeing or hearing his family, Carl began to get scared that they really had been crushed under whatever fell. He waited, staring up at the steep staircase, for his family to return. He killed time chasing cockroaches and trying to catch some of the biting spiders, and then went back and mewed up at the staircase. When he couldn't stay awake any longer, he crept back and curled up in the water-stained and warped cupboard under the long unused sink, finally falling asleep.

Eira heard the rumble and crash coming from the house behind hers. She whipped her head around to look at the house, her blonde ponytail hitting her in the face. She had been going to hide behind the big maple tree, playing hide and seek with her brother Aiden in their backyard, when the noise distracted her and she stopped halfway between the porch and the tree. Then she tripped over her own feet, scuffing her new sneakers with grass stains, as she walked over to the hole in the fence where she could see the back of Mr. Pickering's house, once blue, now sun-bleached and faded.

Despite all the trash, rusted tools, and weather-beaten furniture in his yard, that gap gave a clear look at his back door. Mr. Pickering had so much junk, their dad said his house was probably the same way inside. Maybe something in there had fallen, some pile of stuff he'd stacked too high, like when they played Jenga. Eira had never even seen their weird neighbor, but he always seemed to take in the flyers and door hangers people dropped off, so he must be in there. She always imagined there was some treasure that he had forgotten about or lost. Not like pirate treasure, but like coins or baseball cards or something, where if she found it, she could ask if Mr. Pickering would let her sell it, and she could buy a new board game add-on or something. She was also just curious about what the house looked like inside.

Aiden came up behind her, his eyes wide. His almost white-blonde hair had fallen in front of his eyes so he looked terrified. “What was that?”

“I don’t know,” she said. “It came from Mr. Pickering’s house.”

“Maybe the roof collapsed!” Aiden said, both awed and nervous. He shuffled his feet, then stood on tiptoe, though he was quite small for a five-year-old, and tiptoes weren’t going to change that. He also hadn’t learned how to tie his shoes yet, so Mom still put him in slip-ons or Velcro shoes for playing at home so he couldn’t even get any extra height from his shoes. “No, maybe . . . was it an earthquake?!”

“Earthquakes don’t happen to just one house,” she said, rolling her eyes. “Dad says Mr. Pickering has so much stuff in his house, probably something fell, or a wall collapsed or something.”

Aiden’s eagerness faded. “Is he . . . do you think he’s . . . dead?”

He gulped, his pale, freckled face went even paler, and Eira quickly shook her head so she didn’t scare him any worse.

“Come on, we should go check on him,” Eira said, and she started toward the gate to the front yard so they could walk around to Mr. Pickering's front door.

“W-what?” Aiden looked panicked now. His little eyebrows furrowed and his eyes widened as big as saucers.

“We’ll just knock. If he answers, then we’ll come back home.”

Aiden followed her but stayed a couple steps behind. "Jeff says Mr. Pickering's house is h-haunted."

Eira sighed. Their neighbor Jeff was always trying to scare Aiden because he was so gullible. "Don't worry, Aiden. There's no such thing as ghosts. And Jeff's a butthead."

Mom said not to say that word." Aiden almost looked more shocked at her name-calling than at the idea of having to go knock on the door of a haunted house.

"Mom has called Jeff worse," Eira said. "And anyway, the house isn't haunted. Mr. Pickering just has a lot of stuff and doesn't like people." She knew Aiden needed a little more convincing and had to think of something he couldn't say no to if he did what she asked. "Come on, we can play Mario Kart when we come back, and you can be Yoshi."

Aiden looked up at her like he didn't trust her, but then stuck out his pinky for her to swear with. Eira looped her pinky around his and shook—they had a deal.

As they reached the end of Mr. Pickering's driveway, Aiden did something he hadn't done in a long time—he grabbed Eira's hand. The boys at school had just started telling him girls had cooties, so he didn't hold her hand anymore unless ordered to by their parents or a teacher.

Eira didn't say anything about it, she just walked him up to the door, like they were trick-or-treating instead of checking on their shut-in neighbor who might be trapped under something heavy. She hadn't really felt nervous until they arrived at the doorbell. She was thinking what games she could buy if she found any treasure, but now that they were here, her hand was getting sweaty, and her heartbeat thudded in her ears instead of her chest.

"Do you want to push the doorbell?" she said to Aiden.

Aiden gripped her hand tighter and quickly shook his head. "Do we have to? Maybe we should just t-tell Dad about the crash."

The whole neighborhood seemed to have gone silent—no birds chirping, dogs barking, cars driving past, not even a bug buzzing.

"We're already here," Eira said, more bravely than she felt. She took a deep breath and reached for the button next to the raggedy, wood-and-screen door with most of the paint peeling.

A loud, long *DING-DONG* sounded from deep inside the house, and the harsh noise almost made Eira startle after it was so quiet just a minute ago. Aiden did jump. They waited, and Eira felt her breath get stuck in her chest as she listened for any sound from the house.

"No one's home," Aiden whispered after a few seconds. "Let's go get Dad."

Eira didn't answer; she pressed the bell again. Another deep *DING-DONG* bellowed from behind the door. She waited a few seconds again, and then breathed in deeply to call out, "Mr. Pickering? It's Eira and Aiden Kaveik! Is everything okay? We heard a loud noise!"

Still nothing.

"Let's just go home. Eira, please?" whispered Aiden. His sweaty hand was slipping inside hers now, and the harder he gripped, the slicker it got.

Eira's stomach did a somersault as she thought about going home, getting their dad, but then she thought about that board game, the expensive one their parents wouldn't buy for them, and what treasures might be in Mr. Pickering's house. Would he let them have something if they helped him? She didn't know, but she made up her mind and tried the door. The screen door had only a little hook to keep it shut and it was unlatched. The front doorknob was squeaky, but it gave as she turned it and the door didn't stick when she pushed it open.

"What are you doing?!" Aiden shrieked in his whisper-voice. "What if he's home? We're going to get in trouble!"

"Don't be such a scaredy cat. Anyway, we can explain ourselves. We just wanted to make sure he was okay." She stepped into the house, Aiden's hand still clutching hers. Both of their hands were slippery, and his was shaking.

Eira couldn't believe one person could have so much stuff and couldn't figure why someone would want all *this* stuff in particular. The hallway had stacks of newspapers, what probably amounted to fifty years of *Consumer Reports* magazines, books of all kinds, and loose papers and envelopes piled up against the wall, narrowing the hallway so much that if she and Aiden had been much bigger, they would have had to turn sideways to fit through.

As they walked past the kitchen, Eira thought she heard a little squeak, and she hoped it was her sneaker and not a mouse. Piled up trash bags full of new, never-used kitchen towels, smaller bags, cookbooks, cooking and food magazines filled the room to the point she couldn't get far into it. Careful not to step in any of the pooled garbage juice, spilled soda, or what was probably dried pee from bugs or mice or something, she stood on her tiptoes to try to see around the piles of stuff. She heard the squeak again, and this time, she knew it was not her shoes, but it also didn't sound like a mouse.

Backing out to the hallway, Eira called again, "Mr. Pickering! The front door was open! Are you okay?"

Aiden wrinkled his nose and then pinched it with his free hand. "Ugh, what stinks?"

Eira smelled it, too, and pulled her shirt up over her nose. "Blech, I don't know, something gross. Just pinch your nose and breathe through your mouth." She was pretty sure she knew what it was, but she wasn't going to tell her brother.

Underneath the dust, mothballs, long-standing garbage juice, and rotten food either in or outside the fridge, human, mouse, bug, and who knew what else's pee and poop, Eira smelled something dead. A couple years earlier—Aiden had been too young to remember—a squirrel had died under their back porch, and Dad had to crawl under there to get it out, but it was a very distinct smell. And Eira had unfortunately recently learned in science class that odors were "particulate"—meaning that everything they smelled right now was actually little bits of it in the air—so they were breathing in tiny amounts of poop, dust, rotten food, and the decomposition of something that used to be alive.

The further they got into the house, the worse the clutter became. The floor, even though it was mostly carpeted, was sticky from leaky garbage bags, long-ago spilled drinks, and who knew what else. Most of the walls had some brown and yellow discoloration, and a copper crust and goop had pooled around and out from the baseboards in many places.

Eira didn't think it could even be called clutter—clutter was stuff you could put away, organize. This was just... junk, trash, and broken stuff that didn't belong. As they made their way into what looked like the living room, a dingy recliner stood in the corner and the old boxy TV was on, blaring a staticky cooking show.

"Mr. Pickering?" she called again.

Eira was starting to worry that the dead thing in the house that they were smelling might not be a squirrel or a mouse.

Eira turned and saw that the row of stacked clothes lined against the wall was not made of taller and taller stacks, but was actually hiding a staircase to the second level. Even from far away, she could tell the clothes were all covered in mouse poop. She made a face. This house was so much more disgusting than she imagined, but she was determined to find Mr. Pickering, and maybe still find something that could be called treasure, that was *not* covered in a layer of rodent turds. She started toward the stairs, but Aiden balked.

"I'm not g-going up there!" he whispered urgently. "I want to go home! We should call Dad!"

Eira knew he was probably right, but she couldn't believe someone who had this much stuff didn't have anything that was actually *cool*, and she wanted to find it. Besides, they'd come this far.

"Okay, you go outside and wait for me," she said. "Count to fifty and I'm not back, go get Dad."

By the look on his face, you'd have thought she told *him* to go upstairs while *she* waited outside. His eyes had gotten huge again, and his little hand tightened painfully around hers.

"It'll be okay. Just go count to fifty."

Aiden finally released her hand, turned around and crept back out of the house on his tiptoes until he got out the front door, then he sprinted down the driveway to wait and count.

Eira walked up the stairs, each one creaking under her. Some actually sank a little bit and she hoped if she stepped carefully, she wouldn't fall through. At the top of the stairs, the death stink got worse. Whatever was dead was up here . . . and had been for a while.

The upstairs hallway was crammed full of construction stuff—tiles, carpet samples, paint, and all the tools you'd need for remodeling. Eira stepped over some spilled paint, even though it was long dried, and crept toward what she guessed was the bedroom. She got to a door at the end of the hall and the smell was so bad, she clapped a hand over her nose and mouth, pressing her t-shirt tightly to her face.

Before she pushed open the door, she counted to ten, trying to prepare herself for what she might find—and then remembered Aiden had probably already run home to get Dad. Well, maybe not. Fifty was a lot to count to for a five-year-old.

When she pushed the door open, the rotting smell, nauseating and a little sweet, like overripe fruit or vegetables, overpowered her. Eira couldn't even turn away to throw up but just tossed up her lunch right there. She saw something move on the bed, too fast to register what it was.

The bedroom was not even a place for sleeping anymore. The windows to her left were totally covered in dust, and more piles of clothes and books blocked out most of what little natural light came through. A collection of dirty dishes, TV trays, used paper plates, and takeout containers sat moldering on top of the dresser.

Her gaze fell on the middle of the room, where two tall bookshelves that had been against one wall had fallen forward onto what she assumed was the bed, where little plastic cases of collectible coins had spilled everywhere. Some of the cases had stayed shut, but some had burst open and coins of all denominations, and even some from other countries, spread all over the bed and floor. She was still registering the shelves and their former contents when she saw what was causing the smell. Two massive, bare, hairy feet stuck out past the bookshelves on the bed, gray from decomposition and . . . they were missing toes and flesh, because something had been chewing at them and tearing off little hunks.

Then a little orange kitten emerged from under the fallen bookshelf. She wanted that kitten. She wanted it more than the coins or whatever other treasure might be buried underneath the boxes and clothes and junk in the house. She also felt she had to save the poor thing if it had nothing to eat but a dead man's toes.

She sidestepped her own throw-up, trying to get closer to the bed to grab him, but the kitten arched his back and hissed, a tiny, barely audible sound.

"It's okay, I'm going to get you out of here!" she said, breathing through her mouth as she took another step closer.

The kitten hissed again, and then something else on the bed moved, and the kitten darted away with a clumsy leap off the high bed and scurried under the dresser.

As she took another step closer, Eira saw what the kitten had run from—a snake had slithered out from Mr. Pickering's chest, decomposed and open, and slipped under the bedspread.

Forgetting the kitten, Eira screamed louder than she had ever screamed—even louder than on the upside-down roller coaster last summer—and bolted down the creaky staircase so fast, she forgot to skip the bad step and almost fell. Catching herself with the wobbly railing, she hauled around the corner at the bottom and out the front door as fast as her legs and feet would go.

Aiden was nowhere in sight, but as she rounded the end of the driveway to run up the street, she saw her dad. He was running toward her and scooped her up into his arms. Aiden was white-lipped and shaking a few steps behind.

"Daddy," she sobbed, "Mr. Pickering's dead, and there was a snake!"

"Oh, sweetie." Her dad hugged her tighter than she could ever remember him doing. "You're okay now. It's going to be okay." He didn't set her down or try to walk with her, he just held onto her and let her cry. He stroked the back of her hair, and Aiden had moved closer and wrapped his arms around their dad's leg.

Eira was almost blind from the tears in her eyes that welled and streamed down her face, soaking her dad's t-shirt. She didn't loosen her grip until she heard the siren of a firetruck coming up the street. Her dad put her down and took both her and Aiden by the hand. They backed out of the way so the firefighters could get to Mr. Pickering's house.

"How did they know to come? Did they know Mr. Pickering was dead?" Eira asked.

Her dad's expression changed from soft and comforting to concerned, and he tightened his grip on Eira's hand. "I don't know, sweetie, maybe one of the other neighbors called them."

"Sir," one of the firefighters called, "we're going to need you and your children to move a little farther back while we work."

Their dad nodded and backed up into the street.

"Is this your house?" the same firefighter called. "Do you know if there's anyone else still inside?"

"Mr. Pickering," Eira said, "he's upstairs in the bedroom, but he's . . . he's dead."

The firefighter stood still for a moment, then nodded again. He pressed a button on his radio and said something to the rest of his team that Eira couldn't quite hear. Across the lawn, the firefighters were pulling on big breathing masks before they went into the house, and she wondered if she was going to get sick from going in the house without one of those things on. She felt a sudden tickle in her throat and coughed. Most of the firefighters stayed outside and were walking around the sides of the house and into the backyard, but two of them went inside.

Eira wiped her tears away with the inside of her shirt, pulling it up to dab at her eyes. She realized she was trembling and wrapped her free hand around herself in a half-hug, squeezing her dad's hand tighter with the other. She couldn't see much, couldn't hear their radios, but she couldn't look away. She wondered if the kitten was going to be okay. She hadn't been able to save him, but maybe the firefighters could get to him and get him out of there.

More neighbors had gathered to see what was going on, but everyone stayed behind the firetruck and in the next-door yards on either side so they weren't in the way.

Then, even louder than the crash she and Aiden had heard earlier, a huge, awful groan, like the sound of a tree being cut down when it finally gets to the falling-over point, erupted from the house. All the firefighters came rushing back toward their truck from outside and inside the house. Their dad took a few steps back, pushing Aiden behind him.

The six firefighters reappeared, rushing toward the truck and away from the house. The two that had gone inside the house were covered in dust, and a big whoosh of air and dust escaped through the front door as they opened it.

Eira searched to see if anyone had come out with the little orange kitten, but she didn't see it.

"Daddy? There was a kitten in the house. I couldn't save him," she said, the tears welling up again. "Do you think he's okay?"

Her dad smiled, but he looked sad rather than excited. "Hard to say, Eira. It sounded like something crashed through the floor. They probably won't know until they can go back in there."

"He's so little though, maybe he was able to go under it and run away," she said, hoping the kitten had run away from the noise and made it to safety.

"You could be right. But it's going to take the firefighters a long time to shore up the house and make it safe to go back inside to find Mr. Pickering or anything else."

Eira nodded, and then she had an idea, a brilliant idea. "Maybe we can set some milk and tuna on the back porch and he'll find his way out?"

Her dad smiled at her again but didn't look convinced of the plan. "Sure, honey. I don't think you should get your hopes up, though. He might not be able to smell food that far away, but we can give it a shot."

The house and the walls around Carl shuddered, and the bigger humans tromped out of there way faster than the little girl had. The ceiling over the kitchen fell down. Carl let out a squeak and took cover under the lip of the kitchen cabinets. Dust flooded the room and floated through the light as it settled on all the surfaces and tickled Carl's nose as he breathed.

He took a couple of tentative steps out from under the cabinet, blinking through the dust, and sneezed three times, stumbling sideways as the sneezes escaped. He sat down hard and sniffled, crying out. He didn't think his mom was going to come back this time. And all his brothers and sisters had probably been upstairs, too.

Carl squeaked out a cry again. He was alone. His family was gone. The house, the only place he knew, was falling apart around him. He padded toward the gap in the back door, long ago chewed through by the mice, keeping an eye out for any other incoming dangers. Carl mewed his loudest kitten meow ever in pure terror as he scampered through the hole in the door and out into the unknown outside world.

Hungry, cold, and trembling with fear, Carl crept into the twilight in the backyard, alert to everything around him. Hisses, buzzes, and chitters rose from every corner of the yard, but none seemed to be coming after him. He pattered over to a strip of dirt against the house, drawn by the huge black crickets singing under some overgrown brambly rose bushes. He didn't expect to catch them—he knew his feet weren't quick enough and he wasn't strong enough to jump very far—but he couldn't help pouncing anyway. Then, he froze.

A vaguely familiar but irresistible smell had drifted toward him. He didn't know what it was, but it was food—real, tasty food, not crickets. He kept to the fence, careful not to make a sound, as he followed the aroma. Part of the fence was broken at the bottom and, after checking the other side for anything else scary, he walked straight through.

The grass here was soft under his paws, not like the scratchy weeds and dirt he'd just crossed to get here.

The smell of the food was stronger. Carl felt his stomach growling, pushing him toward the smell. He felt safe in the grass, it rose high enough to conceal him since he was so low to the ground. As hungry as he was, he took his time crossing the grass, still waiting for something to crash down around him or jump out and attack him.

A bird, or some huge thing in the tree overhead, screeched, and Carl raced to get underneath a little chair in the middle of the grass. Breathing so fast, he started to hiccup and toppled backward onto his bottom. He caught his breath again and once he stopped hiccupping and had checked that the bird had moved on to a different yard, he crept back out, still inching his way toward the food.

Finally, he found it. He hadn't eaten all day and stuck his face in the bowl, biting into some kind of fish he had smelled the old man eating before, but that Carl had never tasted. His stomach gurgled in a happy way, and he ate as fast as his jaw would allow. The bowl clean, he moved on to a dish where he lapped up something that tasted sort of like the milk his mother fed him. Eating was tiring, and he stumbled to a little box next to the house. It had a roof and a soft towel inside, and Carl barely got inside before he fell asleep.

When he woke up again, a girl sat next to him on the ground, the same one that had come to the old man's house the day before. She was opening another can of the fish he'd eaten and was adding more milk to the dish. Carl's instincts told him to run and hide, but he didn't see any better refuge nearby, so he just backed up against the back wall of the box. His second instinct was to hiss at her, but maybe he should give her a chance if she was going to keep bringing him food.

Before she got up to leave, she whispered, "Hey, kitty, it's okay. You're safe here."

Carl's ears went back, still unsure if he could trust her, but the girl didn't come any closer or try to bother him. She stood up, left the fish and milk, and went back inside.

Carl waited a long time before he crept out of the box, watching for the girl or anyone else to come back. The sun was coming through the maple tree leaves and creating a nice warm spot on the porch, directly lined up with the bowl of fish. Carl stretched the sleepiness away and padded over to the bowl. As he ate, he realized that over here, at least the house wasn't falling down, and no spiders bit him while he slept.

The One Who Carries Sun-Arrows

Juliana Rew

TAKING A BREAK FROM her training as a goldsmith, Ferryth waded carefully through the shallows of the brackish wetland, seeking shells and colorful corals that she could use in her artwork and writing.

She admired the rays of sunlight illuminating Ailsa Rock, the island sitting in the middle of the firth. The estuary provided both food and shelter for the people living along the Caledonian coast. Behind her, on higher ground, the village settlement hosted chambered tombs holding the bones of her ancestors as well as a great stone circle. She was currently working on artwork for the residents who had passed on to the western shores. Ferryth let her attention slip for only a moment, but that was enough for a stabbing pain to shoot through the sole of her calloused bare foot. It hurt like the *diabhal* and oozed pink blood. She reached down and pulled out the offending object.

She ran her fingers over the prickly surface of the dog winkle. The long-lasting red pigment from the whelk would make a fine addition to her kit of drawing and writing materials. Though Ferryth's tribe still largely made their living as fishermen, they were not immune to the lure of overseas trade, including precious metals, jewelry, and iron weapons. Her own sister had married an Irish lord and abandoned without a second thought the people who loved her, especially Ferryth.

Recently Ferryth felt she had no one. Her parents were both dead, and her two brothers were off to see if they could obtain gainful employment by tagging along with their sister. Well, perhaps she did have one person left—Mona, the dark-skinned witch who taught her to write and draw.

Mona was something of a mystery, since she claimed to have travelled via magic to this place from a land far to the south she called Kemet. Hence, due to the mention of magic, she was immediately labeled a witch. Besides that, she was preternaturally beautiful, which tended to make men act unpredictably. Ferryth admired witches, though they engendered resentment among the superstitious. The fact that Mona had appeared in the middle of the standing stones lent credence to her story.

Ferryth limped to the sandy beach and gathered a poultice from washed up seaweed to soothe her cut foot. At least, she hoped it would soothe. She sat, cradling her foot, while the cries of a flotilla of circling seagulls echoed her despair. They tried to console her, singing sad songs reminding her that they too had lost their mothers.

"Lovely, aren't they?" a voice behind her said. "Nice to see some sunshine instead of the constant drizzle." Startled, Ferryth awoke from the daydream, mere false imaginings that she could understand the language of the birds. Mona patted Ferryth on the back and sat beside her. "We didn't have these pretty little gulls in Kemet, although we did have some handsome herons and ibis. They weren't very smart, though, and their powerful beaks could kill a human." Mona smiled. "You seem to have a knack with animals."

Ferryth shrugged. Maybe you could call it that. She'd inherited some ducks and geese after her family wandered off, and they were more of a chore than a consolation. She had to get up before dawn and scatter grain for them and fill a trough with water. They had gotten domesticated by the ready food supply, so they didn't migrate away in the winter. She didn't like killing the birds, so she occasionally took them to the village butcher and gave him a share of the rendered fat. The meat she sold to others.

"Look, I've brought you some cakes," Mona said. "You're my little vegetarian."

"Your what?" Ferryth said.

“In my culture, these birds would be considered sacred,” Mona said. “Not for eating. Everyone just eats grains and fish and vegetables.”

“I don’t eat fish either,” Ferryth said. “My brothers always stank of them, so I couldn’t face them for dinner.” She thought for a moment. “I didn’t mind cooking them, though.” She wouldn’t mind if her brothers were to come home. On the other hand, they’d probably kill all her animals. They sat eating the oat cakes, which were quite delicious.

“You know, I never asked how exactly you got here.”

“It’s a very long story, kid,” Mona said. “You’d be better off not knowing.”

Suddenly bothered, Ferryth retorted, “I’m not a kid. I’m sixteen, you know. If you don’t trust me, I really don’t know why you claim to be my friend.” She knew that everyone said she was an odd duck. She was taller than all the boys, her streaked brown hair cut short. They didn’t understand either her eating habits or, particularly, her stated occupation as an artist. Lately, when she’d taken up with Mona, they tended not to talk to her at all.

One of her former friends accused her of wanting to rise above her station like her sister. That was completely ridiculous. What would she do with a bunch of servants following her around and cutting into any time she might have to paint and write?

Mona apologized but didn't offer more information, just more mentoring. She had given Ferryth the idea to try some metalworking. "You're quite talented, and you could decorate shields and embellish sword handles to make a tidy living. And it would help you support your animals."

Ferryth looked up, a bit exasperated. "No one would buy a weapon made by a woman," she said.

"Perhaps not, but with a bit of proper buildup, we could make people believe in your work—that it is, in fact, quite desirable."

"You mean put a spell on people? I couldn't do that," Ferryth said.

"Of course not," Mona said. "It would just be a matter of imbuing your creations with a bit of intention."

"What sort of intention?" Ferryth asked, becoming interested. "Like, this sword is intended for a man who wants to make an impression?"

"Exactly," Mona said.

"I was just joking," Ferryth said.

"I wasn't," Mona replied. "See my gold bracelet? The ibis bird symbol on it represents Thoth, the god of writing and wisdom. I learned from the best."

Ferryth had too many orders to fill this week. The village chief was expecting to get his ornate arrow quiver delivered on time. He had even supplied the gold that she was using to emboss the story it bore.

She loved her new occupation and the creativity it afforded, not to mention the money in her pocket, but making other people's projects to order was tricky. Most of them couldn't read, and they were a superstitious lot. So, sometimes she had to explain what the decorations meant and the stories they told.

Mona was a big help with that, luckily. She produced a blank papyrus scroll they could use for practice and taught Ferryth the glyphs used by her own people as well as the stories of the gods of Kemet. Ferryth's tribe had their own gods, of course, but they seemed much more benevolent than Mona's vengeful gods. Still, Ferryth couldn't resist using some of the Kemet gods' symbols and giving them Celtic names. Mona laughed about it, saying, "Imagine people's confusion when they look at these shields and weapons and wonder how Kemet's symbols got on them."

Ferryth just shrugged, too busy to worry about how posterity was going to feel about her creations. She briefly considered skimping on the decorations, since the quiver was just going into the mound of the honored dead alongside the chief's brother. She failed to see what a dead person would need with any gold. *Deid* was *deid*, as far as she was concerned.

Mona dropped by with some of her excellent cakes, undoubtedly to add her critique of Ferryth's work.

"May I?" she said, lifting the quiver and turning it over in her hands. "You missed a spot, here, on the bottom."

Ferryth said she doubted anyone would care.

"On the contrary, my little goldsmith. In my culture, it is important to give gifts that the dead can take along to ensure a happy afterlife."

Ferryth was annoyed by Mona's comment. What if there wasn't any afterlife? It wasn't as if Mona's culture was any better than her own. In fact, her people's burial mounds had existed for a thousand years, even longer than Mona's civilization. She swallowed the harsh retort she was about to make, and thanked Mona instead.

"Thanks, I meant to add some Celtic scrollwork there and hadn't gotten around to it yet."

Mona asked where the chief's brother was going to be laid. The mound was already forty feet high, and there appeared to be no more room for corpses.

"They're digging a new area, and laying a track for giant boulders to be quarried from Ailsa for a foundation. The chief's got everyone cutting trees to use for moving the granite," Ferryth said. "We'll have three mounds when it's all done. And the good news is, the chief has asked me to embellish the walls with the stories of our people."

"Amazing," Mona agreed. "The chief has been very kind to you, making sure you have noble work. I'd be honored to be laid to rest here," she added.

"Don't get your hopes up," Ferryth warned. "You're an outsider, and I'm an odd duck who never fits in."

Mona laughed. “Well, we’ll have to change that, won’t we? When you’re done here, drop by my hut, and we’ll work on your writing. If you’re going to tell the stories of your people and make them last, you’re going to have to hone your craft to become an expert storyteller.”

Once again, Ferryth felt slightly annoyed. She already knew the stories of her people, handed down orally through the generations. All she had to do was write them down. What was so hard about that?

Writing stories turned out to be more difficult than Ferryth expected. Part of the problem was finding time to work on them. Then, when she was ready to paint the glyphs, there was no place to paint them.

The new funeral mound was far from finished. A jumble of boulders and logs splayed around the meadow adjoining the other two mounds. Fog and rain had begun, signaling the onset of autumn. People harvested grain and dried fish for the winter over smoky peat fires. The witch Mona wandered from house to house, offering advice on food preservation. More than once, a housewife spat on the ground after Mona had left.

Ferryth made her way down the muddy path, carrying the golden quiver to the chief’s hut to get paid in flour, assuming he approved. He only nodded and told her to hold onto it until the tombs were ready. “I have a version of the story for your brother’s tomb ready,” she said. “Do you want me to read it to you?”

The chief scowled. "I don't know why I let that witch talk me into having pictures and writing inside the new hillock. We never needed that before. And putting tunnels through the hill just means there is less room to put those waiting to pass to the western isles. But I found it hard to turn down her requests, and I have to agree that they will make the funeral mound more impressive."

Surprised, Ferryth said nothing, not wishing to encourage further animosity toward Mona. The villagers were perfectly willing to bury treasures and gold, but they didn't want to put up with a little writing? She was coming around to Mona's opinion that history was a good thing. Just as good as tradition in its own way. She exited the chief's hut and decided to return to her own for a flax bag. She'd head for the woods to pick some tasty brambles, which were well worth the bloody fingers. Maybe she'd get some new ideas for stories.

Ferryth's workshop was also her bedroom. Just outside was an open fireplace where she could smelt metals and pour them into molds she had devised for small items like beads and pendants. She had banked the firepit to protect it from the wind and keep sparks from setting her little hut afire. The protective rock ring made it easy to stoke in the mornings. Right now, however, her hut was freezing cold, about the same temperature as the outdoors. She wrapped herself in the grey woolen blanket that her mother, an expert weaver, had made.

That, and the flap of felted wool that covered her doorway served as her only souvenirs from family life. Too bad the shawl wasn't as tightly woven as her mother's blanket, but she'd soon be asleep until it was time to step outside and stoke the fire once again.

She heard footsteps outside her entrance and rose to investigate. She'd brought all her precious metals inside, so any thief would find slim pickings.

"Ferryth, are you home?" Mona called.

Sighing, Ferryth put aside the blanket and pulled open the flap. It was snowing.

"What is it?" Ferryth asked.

Mona pushed her way in, shivering. "By the gods, it's cold. I need to leave something with you." She pulled a scroll from under her shawl. "It's the key to the symbology of my people."

"Why do you want me to have it?" Ferryth asked.

"Because I stole it, and they're looking for me."

"And you want me to hold stolen goods? What if they come here?"

Mona explained that she had a method for enchanting the scroll so that only Ferryth could read it. She was to copy the writing onto another scroll using vinegar as ink, then burn the original. The resulting scroll would contain writing, but it would be invisible, unless you added a second ingredient to the papyrus. She held up a vial of alum powder.

"In Kemet, we collected this powder from the western desert and used it in cooking."

"That doesn't sound like a very well-kept secret, if you ask me," Mona's student sniffed. "Besides, why don't you just do that yourself?"

"As I explained, they're after me. I have to leave immediately. I suggest you get to work."

"Leave? Why? Who's after you?" Ferryth was shocked. She knew people didn't like Mona much, but she didn't expect them to persecute her.

"You're a big, tall girl," Mona said, putting her arm around Ferryth. "You can take care of yourself. You've been doing it all along."

Ferryth's face crumpled into the makings of a sob.

"Don't be such a baby," Mona said. "If it'll make you feel any better, you can have my bracelet as a keepsake. Oh, I've left some suggestions for the funeral mound stories. It'll be a great way to preserve the stories, because hardly anyone will tamper with them. Maybe in a few centuries, it'll be worth coming back."

"A few centuries?" Ferryth said.

"Goodbye, little chick," Mona said. Ferryth turned away to wipe some inconvenient tears. A sharp snapping sound caused her to look back to her friend and teacher. It was only the wind, pushing the door flap closed.

When spring returned, the weather was hardly better, but at least work resumed on the third mound. No one was interred there yet, and several who had died over the winter, including the chief's brother, waited for the completion of their final earthly resting place. Ferryth had copied Mona's glyph key and hidden the scroll, now folded flat, on the floor under her bed. The longer days allowed her to study the original for the first time since Mona had left. She'd burn it afterwards, as promised.

The scroll contained few stories, but the key glyphs it held were strange. They evoked lightning and thunder from the heavens, as well as war and darkness. Tall humanlike beings, presumably hostile gods, crushed humans in their path and burned their homes to ashes. Kemet's gods fell before them as well, including Mona's powerful mentor, Thoth. Stars fell from the skies.

Although she felt it alarming to destroy the original scroll, Ferryth hurried to complete its destruction. These glyphs might be portents. She felt depressed about the loss of her friend, but she tried to use the lessons she had been taught to write her village's stories and to devise inscriptions for the treasures to be left with the dead. She combed through the story suggestions Mona had left, feeling heartened that the witch felt they were worthy of preserving. Maybe Ferryth's people's stories could prevent the disasters Mona's scroll seemed to foretell.

One of her newest creations was the quiver that would accompany the grave of the chief's brother, inscribed with an advanced glyph that Mona taught her: "The One Who Carries Sun-Arrows."

The mound grew gradually, built around a central open area accessible by a single doorway outside. Inside, the villagers dug tunnels in a star shape. The walls inside the "star mound," as it came to be called, contained small corpse-sized alcoves that would eventually house the remains of the entire village and probably their children and grandchildren.

Word spread about the spectacular funeral mound project, and visitors from remote areas came to study it. The chief, always suspicious of the strangers, showed up at Ferryth's hut one day as she filled orders for memorials.

"There's one of those people like the witch Mona poking around here," he said. "He demanded a tour of the star mound."

"Really?" Ferryth was excited at first, but then she remembered Mona's words: "They're after me." She wondered if this was the "they" Mona had talked about. Wiping her hands on her leather apron, she said, "Interesting. Let me get finished here, and I'll come along shortly."

Ferryth scanned the sky. The moon was rising, time to quit for the day. She decided to take the easy way and rake the rocks into a pile to kill the fire. Anxious to see this intriguing visitor, she set off toward the star mound, leaving the village behind. Her feet picked up stacks of mud, which she ignored until they grew so heavy she could no longer lift her legs. Stopping briefly to scrape off a couple inches of clay, she regretted not taking a walking stick, which would have served multiple purposes: scraper, cane, and weapon, if needed.

"You are the scribe Ferryth, I take it?" a voice behind her said. She jumped. The person was of Mona's people, dark, with curling black hair. He had a small goatee beard and quite a bit longer nose.

"Our chief said you were looking for me," Ferryth replied.

The stranger introduced himself as Thoth, noting he was an admirer of scribes and purveyor of knowledge.

"You can't fool me so easily, stranger," Ferryth said. "Thoth is a god, and you are certainly not. I am not so gullible."

The stranger's head grew smaller, his long nose longer, until it resembled the beak of one of the marshland herons. Ferryth swallowed, terrified. It appeared she had been mistaken about the stranger's identity. Now she understood.

"What do you want with me? she asked.

"Your friend Mona stole something that belongs to me. A scroll. Do you have it?"

"I'm afraid you're too late," Ferryth said. "Mona left a while ago, and I have no scroll."

With his forefinger, the stranger drew some runes in the sod, flames licking the edges. Loosely translated, they said:

"The One Who Carries Sun-Arrows"

Thoth's voice grew louder. "That rune is forbidden to you. You cannot have learned that phrase except from me or Mona. Where is the scroll?"

Ferryth was loyal to her friend, but more than that, she was stubborn.

"Go away, you demon-headed monster. You are not one of my people's gods, and I'll write what I please."

"You are indeed a very talented metalsmith and scribe, but you are foolish to believe Mona's lies. I usually rather enjoy thieves, they're amusingly resourceful, but in this case, humans are not yet ready for the knowledge on that scroll. You're ahead of the destined timeline for metalloid-based knowledge. The rune for silicon is especially forbidden to you."

Ferryth only crossed her arms to keep them from trembling.

"I don't have time to argue with silly mortals like you," Thoth said. "You have been warned." He pulled a hood over his head and vanished.

Ferryth fell to her knees. Gods were real, and she just met one! Her heart raced, and she knew she had to put the scroll somewhere safer than under her bed. She would hide it in the star mound, along with the stories of her people she had been writing. The mound was too huge for even a god to breach. She hurried back home and slipped the folded scroll under her shawl. Outside, she heard a call from her ducks, "kwa, kwa—stay, stay." With a backward glance, she promised to feed her animals—later.

As she entered the mound, Ferryth heard the rumble of thunder and was nearly trampled by two workers running out.

The chief followed, shouting, “Get home, Ferryth. There’s been a cave-in, and the mound is collapsing.”

Ferryth saw that the mound hadn’t collapsed completely yet. There was still hope of burying Mona’s scroll. “I’ll be there soon,” she answered, heading farther inside the mound, until she came to the chamber reserved for the chief’s brother, which held the gold quiver.

That evening, the chief announced that the great star mound was no more. No one had died in the disaster, except probably Ferryth. “She was slow to turn back, saying she just had to add one more touch to my brother’s memorial.” He ran his fingers through his thinning hair. “She was very dedicated,” he added. “She was like a daughter to me.”

Present Day

Led by prominent archeologist Dr. Mona Mohamed, scientists on the coast of western Scotland discovered the buried rubble of an ancient Celtic ruin, a nearby village, and a site used for smelting iron and precious metals. Dictating a description of the Neolithic find into her mobile device, Dr. Mohamed reported: “ . . . only a few bodies, probably a ruined Iron Age funeral mound. The mound has a single entrance, where we found the corpse of a woman. She was unusually tall for the era and wore a bracelet with what appears to be an Egyptian hieroglyph of the god Thoth. She is holding a sheaf of arrows covered in gold leaf, an especially fine example of Iron Age workmanship.”

Wearing white gloves, Dr. Mohamed picked up the quiver and reached inside. Her assistant gasped and asked what she was doing. Mohamed pulled out a folded papyrus document.

"Aha, as I suspected, there's a hidden scroll. Some of it appears to have been written with invisible ink," Mohamed said.

"How do you know that?" her assistant asked. Without replying, Mohamed placed the document into a sample box and asked that it be submitted for further analysis.

Six months later, Dr. Mohamed's scholarly article in the *Oxford Journal of Archaeology* detailed the results of the preliminary analysis. The summary concluded with the statement: "Our original theory that the markings inside the scroll were ancient glyphs appears to be correct based on comparisons with Middle Eastern rock paintings. My colleagues and I came to the surprising conclusion that the scroll consists of a palimpsest of ancient Egyptian hieroglyphs, combined with advanced scientific and technical knowledge, including electricity. We are especially thrilled that it mentions the Library of Alexandria, which is said to have housed all of the knowledge of the ancient world. This is stunning evidence of an Egyptian-European connection from more than two millennia ago.

"The script claims that it is the property of the ancient Egyptian god, Thoth, but we doubt that that is entirely accurate. The majority of information here seems to have been added at a later date, by a Celtic scribe who called herself Ferryth. Her beautiful golden quiver somehow survived millennia and preserved the stories and lives of her people. She deserves to be credited and revered."

Carrion Souls

Ian K. long

THE HIGH TREE branches clicked in the cold winter air like dry bones. Jayden had never been to this part of Rucksaw Woods. This area, no bigger than a baseball infield, was all dirt with no sign of vegetation. Tall oaks with winter darkened bark surrounded the space like the walls of an arena, making Jayden feel small. And while the presence of the ten-foot-tall pillar of stone, smack dab in the middle, brought the creep factor to a boiling point, he didn't want to wimp out in front of Brody. Especially since they'd spent all of yesterday morning in seventh grade homeroom, planning their trip to the Devil's Circle.

"My brother brought me here last week," Brody said. "He tells me nothing ever grows here. Not even during the summer."

"And I thought the old silo was creepy." Jayden brushed his brown bangs from his eyes.

"Yeah." Brody nodded. "Rucksaw Woods is filled with places like this."

They loved exploring old ruins. Had ever since the fifth grade. And each year their exploits became bolder and more daring.

A howl of wind ripped through the treetops of the infertile ring they stood inside.

"When I came here last week with my brother, I saw all sorts of weird shit."

"Like what?" Jayden asked.

"People in old timey clothes."

"You mean like ghosts?" Jayden asked.

"No. More like, images in my head. Flashbacks of what it was like here, long ago. I could hear voices, too. One that yelled, *go away!*" Brody scanned the area nervously. Shaking his head. "You've heard of Matron Skole, right?"

Anyone in the town of Crenlin, New Jersey, knew the Matron's story. The sprawling Skole Estate had an orphanage, living quarters for the staff, and Matron Skole's small stone cottage.

"Yeah," Jayden said. "She ran a children's home a long time ago. Murdered twenty some orphans?"

Brody scratched the soil with a stick he had found. "And got away with it by claiming every missing kid was just another runaway. But there's another part of her story you may not have heard about."

Jayden listened to Brody recount the legend and was surprised to see the Matron in his mind just like Brody had said.

1880

Sitting in the armchair of her study, Matron Skole admired the red-hot glow of embers popping and sizzling in the fireplace. This stone cottage was her sanctuary away from the orphanage, and the bottle of whiskey on the end table was her silent companion for the night. She could feel the tension in her jaws relax while tipping the glass tumbler to her lips. With the cold of the night invading her home, she got up and put another log in the fireplace.

Three loud knocks came at the door when she was about to sit back down. The peaceful fire's light flickered off the frame. No news from her staff at this hour was good news.

Three more knocks. She unlatched the thumb bolt, expecting a long rant from her assistant about misbehaving boys, but her breath caught in her throat when six-year-old William Crawford stood before her. An impossibility because she had killed him a year ago, the same way she did to any kid that stood up to her.

Her heart raced in her chest at the sight of the black orbs that replaced his eyes.

"Please." It was William's voice, only tinny and echoey. With his arms folded across his chest and hands wedged underneath his armpits his teeth chattered. "I'm freezing. And I'd like to come inside."

Except for his eyes, everything about him matched. He even wore the same clothes she'd buried him in, only these were impossibly pristine and clean—a blue velvet vest, a white button-down shirt, grey knickers, black socks, and black boots.

Her lips quivered. "Dear Lord Jesus." She'd never known booze to cause hallucinations. "Go away."

"I just need to warm up," the boy said. "Please."

A loud pop from the log catching fire caused her to jump, but she then regained what composure she had.

"Away!" she yelled. "Leave!"

The boy leaned forward, took in a long sniff, and smiled. His voice changed to a guttural, gravelly tone.

"Your soul is all wrong." With a half grin, he squinted, his black eyes glinting in the fire's light. Then he said, "Dead." The single word showed off his perfect teeth.

While closing the door on the creature's face, she yelled, "Leave!" Only the door thudded instead of slammed shut as two little hands with black clawed fingers clasped the edge of the frame. An arctic chill snaked in from outside as the demon boy's face pressed against the crack of darkness, its black eyes staring into hers.

With its putrid breath of rotting flesh, it whispered, "I'm going to put my seed into ya, wench."

Swinging the door back open, she kicked the demon in the gut, but it didn't budge. Instead, it pulled from its vest pocket a black jeweler's box, just like the one William used to have, a keepsake given to him by his mom. The demon opened it and smoke as dark as its eyes leaked from its ears, nose, and mouth and poured into the box.

Slamming the door shut and latching the lock, Matron Skole slid to the floor in a crouch.

"Dear God." She rocked back and forth. "Just an aberration."

She gathered herself. The fire illuminated the amber liquid she now yearned for more than ever. After a shot of whiskey, she opened the door and was relieved to find the boy gone. But the black box sat like a wart on her stoop. She picked it up with the intention to throw it as far from her cottage as possible. When she pulled back to throw, the box yanked from her grip and fell to the floor as the door slammed shut. The small container opened. Black tendrils slipped over the top of the box and dropped to the floor like a heavy fog. The malignant mass of darkness coalesced into a single serpentine shape and slithered up her leg. Repulsed and terrified, she gripped her groin, slid to the floor, and blacked out.

Brody kneeled, jamming the stick into the ground. He locked eyes with Jayden. "Nine weeks later she gave birth."

"You mean nine months?"

"No." Brody shook his head. "Weeks."

The image of Matron Skole flashed to Jayden's mind. Her legs spread apart. The doctor at the foot of her bed. Everything like a waking dream, every detail as clear as reality with Brody's voice now a distant echo.

The doctor's top hat and leather travelling medical bag sat on a steamer chest. Sunlight streamed through the window of the bedroom. Matron's assistant stood by the doctor, who said, "Push!"

Jayden had seen the birth of a child in sex ed clips where the baby's head breaches. Only instead of a head, three tiny, clawed fingers forming a birdlike hand slipped through the opening of the birth canal and gripped to one side. "Holy God!" the doctor yelled and backed away. The second birdlike hand, grey in color, emerged. Bigger than a newborn's fingers and impossibly strong, they spread apart the vaginal opening. While the assistant prayed, Matron Skole screamed in agony. "Get it out of me!" A small head crowned and pulled a black viscous mucus away from the birth canal. The demon craned its face upward, exposing its black eyes and fanged teeth.

Fully out now, this demon arched its back like a cat.

Brody's voice became clearer, and less distant.

"They couldn't kill it," Brody said.

"Just take a bat to its face." Jayden's heart beat in his head.

"Not possible."

The fiend scuttled along the floor, its arms as long as its hindquarters. The doctor drew his Colt revolver from his leather carrying case and pulled the trigger, but his hand jerked, and the gun fired left. After a frenzy of screams and yells and items thrown, the creature plastered itself in the corner of the ceiling like a belfry bat. The doctor pulled over a chair and stood upon it, placing his gun up to the creature's head.

Exhausted, Matron Skole clutched the fireplace mantle, noting the ridged bumps of the thing's spine, its pale grey skin, pointed ears, and what looked like the growth of small wings underneath its armpits. She shivered at the thought of this coming from her body.

The fiend breathed in fast succession with its eyes closed while Matron Skole waited for the resounding blast of gunfire that would end its life.

"I can't do it," the doctor gasped.

"What do you mean?" Even after the agony of labor, she'd shoot this evil firstborn herself.

"My finger won't move."

"Get down," she demanded.

Clutching the chair, she gestured for the doctor's gun.

"Give it here! Come on!" She stared him down until he relented.

Her finger touched the cool metal of the trigger, but . . . "Damn it!" She couldn't will her finger to move.

The doctor exited the room. More clatter arose from the bedroom while the doctor told the Matron's assistant to help him. Within seconds, they placed the Matron's now empty steamer chest underneath the sleeping demon.

"Give me that broom," the doctor said with his hand outstretched.

He wedged the broom handle underneath the creature, and like prying a cat clawing a sweater, plopped it into the steamer chest and shut it. The creature woke, screeching, thudding, and banging against the inside of the steamer chest.

Sitting on top, he asked, "Matron, do you have a key?" When he didn't get a response, he yelled, "The key, damn it!"

"In the top drawer of my dresser!" she said.

The doctor turned to the assistant and demanded. "Grab it!"

Within seconds, the Matron's assistant returned with the key and locked the steamer chest. They wrapped rope from one side of the chest to the other and back, tying the ends into a secure knot. The creature continued to ram against the walls with tremendous force while both the assistant and the doctor wrestled the steamer chest out of the cottage. After loading it onto the doctor's buggy, they rode to St. Rose Church down the street to alert Father Callahan.

"We ride deep into those woods and bury it alive," Father Callahan said. "God will take care of the rest."

No one disagreed.

The baying wails and hisses faded with every shovel full of dirt that filled the unhallowed grave. When done, they stomped down the soil with their feet and patted the area with their shovel blades. The howls and hisses became a muffled baby's cry.

"Every night before bed, she'd hear those cries," Brody said. "And every day for a month, she blessed the grave with Father Callahan's holy water."

"Did the cries stop?" Jayden asked.

"Kinda." Brody traced the tip of his walking stick along some permafrost cracks in the ground before him.

"What do you mean?" Jayden asked. "By kind of?"

"One day she came back to the grave and there was a hole."

"It crawled out?" Jayden asked.

Matron Skole approached the now disturbed grave of rocks and dirt piled off to the side of a gaping hole. Her heart dropped just as a shadow passed her feet.

High above, the giant avian terror dove down like a hawk, the membrane of its translucent batwings red and veiny in the daylight. In a single hit, it knocked her down, pinned her shoulders to the ground, and bore its black eyes into hers.

"No. Please." She trembled while its stare turned from dark black to a glowing hot red. "God, please!"

"Father Callahan found her mangled body in a field not too far from here. Practically all her bones were broken, like she'd been beaten to death." A loud snap off in the woods caught both boys' attention. They froze and stared wide-eyed with white faces. Brody gulped before continuing.

"Matron Skole was the Crenlin Devil's first victim. Since then, there have been forty in all. Mr. Trembly was the last."

"Mr. Trembly," Jayden said the name aloud, realizing five months had passed since his death. "I forgot about him. He was a Boy Scout leader at one point."

"Yeah. My dad led a troop when my older brother was twelve and says Trembly is why scout leaders get a bad rap. That creep had a thing about young boys, and my dad considered his death karma. Anyway, the police found Trembly's body bludgeoned to death in a field."

"They're all found that way, huh?" Jayden said. "Every victim, somehow crushed. Who can do something like that?"

"Nothing human." Brody shook his head and gulped. "My brother tells me that true monsters are beasts, born from darkness and pure evil."

A shiver skittered down Jayden's spine.

They stood a moment in silence. Then Brody asked, "Can you feel that?"

Jayden nodded. "Like something's watching us?"

"Yeah. These woods are all wrong."

Brody checked his watch before running his stick along the shadow cast by the stone pillar. "Every day at three-thirty, this shadow points northeast, the direction of the next place I want to show you."

They hiked to a craggy rock path that led to a cliff.

Brody gestured ahead of them. “That’s Satan’s Perch.”

Jayden followed Brody to the natural rock structure that jutted over a deep ravine and a raging river. Dizzy, he backed away and stumbled on a climber’s bolt.

Kneeling, Brody fiddled with a carabiner attached to the bolt. “Not too many climb here anymore.”

“Why?”

“This spot has a lot of bad juju.”

The natural stone plank was a bit wider than a diving board and extended three feet over the edge.

“This place is just as creepy as The Devil’s Circle,” Jayden said.

“Yeah.” Brody picked up a rock and tossed it over the edge. It tumbled through the air before plunging into the river. “The Crenlin Devil has a lair right below us in the cracks of this cliff. And just like a bat, it comes out at night.”

That same excited chill Jayden experienced at Halloween washed over him. But the air was also tainted like in the dead clearing.

“Sacrifices are done here,” Brody said, as if to prove that point.

“Human?” Jayden gulped.

“No.” Brody nudged his foot on the climber’s bolt. “Animals. Mostly dogs.”

He pointed to two small blood-stained trenches carved into the stone that extended outward from the climber’s bolt in a V-shape.

"The blood runs right over the cliff's edge," Brody explained.

Jayden couldn't help thinking of his own dog, Duke. "Why, though?"

"My brother says these wackos think if they do enough animal sacrifices, the Crenlin Devil will show up to make a pact with them."

Jayden tried to push away the thought of Duke being sacrificed, but the splinter of an idea needled at him, toyed with him, and even laughed at him until a crushing sorrow made him want to get home to make sure his dog was safe.

"That's disgusting," Jayden said. "And they just keep killing until it shows up?"

"Yeah. Of course if the sacrifices were human, that would be blood in the water, and would for sure get the Crenlin Devil's attention."

Jayden pulled out his phone and tapped the app that kept tabs on where his dog was through a tracker attached to Duke's collar. The pinwheel turned while the app took forever to load and the woods around him grew more menacing.

Fear gripped him when the app showed his dog not at home.

Brody asked, "You okay?"

"I'm fine," he lied.

Logically, he knew there was little chance these rumored demon worshippers had targeted his dog, but it still felt possible with this dark juju. Furthermore, his dog's Houdini-like ability to escape from home didn't help with this sudden anxiety.

Jayden felt trapped underneath the high branches that sprawled across the red evening sky like a giant spider's web.

"Sorry." Jayden attempted to stop trembling. "But I don't really want to be here anymore."

"Nah, man." Brody shrugged his shoulders. "It's cool. To be honest, I'm creeped out, too, like something's been watching us this whole time."

"Yeah," Jayden gulped.

They parted on foot after leaving the Rucksaw Woods, and Jayden was relieved the app showed Duke a quarter of a mile away at the city park. Not uncommon for his dad to take his dog there, he knew.

The mercury lamps of the park washed away some of the muddy darkness.

He ran up to the parental silhouette ahead. "Dad!"

But when he got closer his stomach crunched in confused panic. He found some guy wearing camo playing with his dog.

"Duke!" Jayden hollered. "Come here, boy!"

Obediently the big brown Rhodesian Ridgeback trundled up and dropped a stick at his feet, wagging with excitement. Jayden rubbed the top of Duke's smooth head.

"What are you doing with my dog?" he demanded, though his heart thumped in his chest when he saw it was Lars Keller, a community creep who, after serving a year in prison for arson, now worked at the local quarry.

"What's it look like?" The mercury lamp cast one side of the creep's face in shadow. "I'm playing fetch."

"He's not your dog," Jayden said.

"Isn't playing fetch what people do with dogs?" He approached Jayden, kneeled and scratched Duke behind the ears. "Such a perfect dog," Lars said, his emerald eyes stone cold in the lamp's light. "So friendly. So harmless. So perfect." His words crystallized in the cold air with a dark menace.

Snapping out of his catatonic state, Jayden grabbed Duke's collar and yanked him away. "I said, he's not your dog."

Locking eyes with Jayden, Lars said, "I know where you live."

Jayden opened his mouth to say something but before he could, Lars spoke again.

"And I was going to return him to you."

Sure you were, Jayden thought.

Lars stared at Jayden a long moment before saying, "I saw the very thing you guys were looking for earlier." The creep's razor thin lips creased into a sideward grin. "Saw it tonight. The Crenlin Devil. Such a powerful beast. Anyway, I'll see you like I always do." He lumbered off into the shadows.

"Jesus!" Jayden's pounding heart reverberated in his head. "Stay away from him, Duke. You hear?"

Duke whined and chuffed. Jayden took a few seconds to calm himself the best he could but startled again when his phone buzzed.

"Duke, sit!" Jayden reached into his coat pocket.

His mom had texted him. Just as he swiped the screen, something eclipsed the moon, causing Duke to tug hard before breaking free and bolting away.

"No! Duke! Come back! Now!"

Duke headed toward the Rucksaw Woods, and the hunt was on. Through waist high meadow, Jayden chased his dog. Damn it, Duke! Why?!? He cursed in his head.

A giant bird, too big for a night owl, flew past Jayden, its shadow gliding over the grassy plains. Duke barked at the night flyer, which flew ahead and circled back, now looking similar to a pterodactyl. No doubt the Crenlin Devil, this thing had to have had a wingspan of at least fifteen feet.

Over the hill, the old grey silo loomed like a giant tombstone. Jayden's neckline tingled with the beast in pursuit right behind him, its batlike wings leathery, yet flapping with an eagle-like grace. It whooshed by, causing him to stumble. Jayden rolled onto his back and a burst of wind flashed at his face as the beast landed, pinning him down with its talons. He could feel the energy of the Crenlin Devil as its black eyes bore into him, searching his mind, plucking away at memories and his past. Shutting his eyes to avoid the stare and prepare for certain death, he felt the Crenlin Devil lunge. Cringing, he waited for the beast to gouge his eyes, but the dark creature now thrashed its wings in pursuit of something else. Duke! Jayden sprang to his feet. The meadow's grass parted in the wake of the malignant silhouette that suddenly dove beneath the high brush like an osprey.

Three deer scattered through the brush, and above, the Crenlin Devil churned its wings with massive effort and gained considerable altitude, holding something in its clasp.

"No!" Jayden yelled as fear and sadness gripped him. His dog, his lifelong friend, gone.

A loud bark came from the fields. Fumbling with his phone in nervous hope, he saw a dot indicating Duke was only ten yards away. Confused but relieved, Jayden ran toward the ping.

The Crenlin Devil released what must have been a deer that plummeted to the ground in a dreadful thud. Jayden gripped Duke in a hug. A low guttural growl rumbled from his dog's chest as the beast swooped in and fed on its kill. The bright moon's light reflected off the sheen of its bat wings and scaly body.

Clutching Duke's collar, Jayden backed away, no longer questioning his belief in monsters or where Brody's brother claimed they came from.

When he got home, he immediately texted Brody:

You'll never believe what I just saw . . .

That next evening, with his parents out to dinner, Jayden had the house to himself.

Normally, he'd revel in these times of independence, but since last night, he yearned for the company of adults.

He took some comfort gaming online with Brody and was surprised how much time had passed since his parents had left. Pausing a moment, he sauntered into the kitchen, noting a chill in the air. The mudroom door leading to the garage was wide open.

Duke had managed to maneuver the door's lever handle, the way he always did, and his parents had forgotten to close the garage door.

"Shit!" He looked at his phone, expecting Duke to be close by and for the dog wrangling to be quick. However, Duke had journeyed back to the fields. "Shit!" When he saw Duke's signal not moving, the Crenlin Devil sprang to mind, along with Duke lying dead in a field, his bones crushed from impact.

No way was he going out there alone this evening. Jayden texted Brody.

Meet me at City Park was Brody's response.

While they trudged through the fields, Jayden checked his phone; Duke was a thousand feet away. The closer they got, the more Jayden wanted to run to the spot while also fearing what he might discover.

"We'll find him," Brody said. "He's in these fields somewhere. It'll be okay."

Jayden wasn't so sure.

The silhouette of the abandoned silo pressed against the dark sky. Knowing he was close, Jayden checked his phone. The ping came from inside the silo.

Pointing at the structure, Jayden shivered at the thought of entering. "I forget how to get in."

Brody shook his head and gulped. "Around the back."

On the other side, the graying structure bathed in the moon's light with the boys' shadows, phantomlike, flitting across the high brush.

"You really want to do this?" Brody asked.

Jayden swallowed. On the verge of tears he said, "You can stay here if you want, but I have to."

Brody shook his head. "You're not going in alone." He turned his phone's flashlight on, squatted, and crawled through a small square opening in the silo.

With dread pulling at his heart, Jayden followed. Inside, the signal was ten feet away.

"Duke?" Jayden's echoing voice startled him.

In the middle of the abandoned silo sat a piece of plywood angled as if lying on top of something. Duke, Jayden thought. It couldn't be anything else. He flung the plywood over and was relieved to find the dog tracker resting on a cinderblock.

"It must have fallen off," Jayden said.

Then, twisting like a coiled snake in his stomach, a new fear of never finding Duke again emerged.

A sudden bright light cast their shadows against the curved silo wall in front of them. Jayden turned, and the headlamp stung his eyes.

"This complicates things." Lars shook his head. "Didn't expect two of you."

Petrified, Jayden managed to squeak, "Don't hurt my dog."

"Heh," Lars chuffed. "That stupid mutt is the least of your worries."

Lars reached to the side of his belt and grabbed a gun.

"Drop your cellphones."

Brody's mouth hung agape. He froze.

"Now!"

They discarded their phones like weapons.

Placing his revolver up to Jayden's back, he turned to Brody. "You exit first. And if you run, I shoot your friend."

Once outside the silo, Lars signaled with his revolver. "Walk in that direction until I tell you otherwise."

Jayden followed Brody into the woods. While Lars guided them, Jayden tried to come up with some sort of plan. He had no idea until one measly thought surfaced. Get a rock as a weapon, which should be the easiest thing to find out here, but he could see none in the headlamp's light. Up ahead, the moon caught something bright. With his luck, it would turn out to be a spongy mushroom, but he'd have to take that chance. He fake-tripped, grabbed the stone, and in a single movement, placed it into his jacket pocket.

"Get up, dumbass!" Lars said.

Jayden dusted himself off and resisted the urge to throw the rock right at the creep's head. He'd only been to Satan's Perch once, but he knew that's where they were headed. The frozen dirt crunched beneath their shoes and the trees creaked and popped in the quiet landscape that looked so different at night. This excursion felt different, too. Unlike yesterday, where exploration brimmed with a tinge of daring and controlled fear, this was a march to certain death. Moreover, guilt swelled heavy in his stomach for having dragged Brody into this mess in the first place.

"Stop," Lars said.

The boys froze in their tracks as if participating in a sadistic game of Simon Says. Backs crawling, they waited for his next command.

"A thing of beauty." He pointed.

With its distinct batwings, pronounced neck, and long tail, the Crenlin Devil glided high above the treetops. Jayden would be fine never seeing it again. Hell, at this point, he'd be fine never seeing the outside of his bedroom.

"Woo! Tonight might be my lucky night." Lars aimed his gun at a 45-degree angle. His salute shot ripped through the evening sky.

The guy was batshit crazy.

Within minutes, they reached Satan's Perch. Above, the Crenlin Devil pulled its wings through the air a few times before diving into the canyon, perhaps into its cliffside lair.

Duke, still alive but whimpering, was chained to the carabiner Jayden had tripped over yesterday. He wanted to cry at the sight of his dog and resisted every temptation to run up and hug him.

"You." Lars gestured to Brody with his gun. "Walk out to the end of Satan's Perch."

Jayden's stomach dropped.

Brody gulped. "I—"

Jayden gripped the stone in his coat pocket. The millisecond Lars let his guard down was the one in a million chance Jayden had to connect a rock to his foe's head. The only chance. The blow wouldn't be fatal, but he just wanted to go home, hopefully with both his friend and dog alive.

"March!" Lars demanded, aiming his gun at Brody, whose moonlit eyes widened in fear.

His friend turned and shuffled out to the edge of the plank with his rounded shoulders shaking like a leaf.

"Please don't kill me," he said.

Lars placed the gun to the back of Brody's head. Shock thundered through Jayden like a gunshot had already been fired. And it may as well have, they were both as good as dead.

"I don't want to die," Brody begged.

"Sorry," Lars said. "But I only need one of you."

Jayden's heart dropped while he clutched the rock in his grip. Throw the rock now, he demanded his brain. But his body froze in fear.

Lars brought the gun down to his side.

"Waste of a bullet, if you want my opinion," he said, his breath lingering in the cold air with his words.

Jayden could feel his Adam's apple move up and down as he gulped, with life around him lurching to a stop. In that moment, the weirdest thought occurred to him, his parents finishing up their meal and peaceful date. Then as if unpausing everything around him, a shooting star streaked silently across the sky, an owl hooted, and Lars shoved Brody over the edge.

Dropping to his knees, Jayden yelled, "No! What did you do? No!"

Lars turned and faced him. "I told you." He smiled casually with his fist to his hip like he'd done nothing at all. "I had no need for him." He stepped off Satan's Plank. "You, on the other hand . . ."

Duke, who'd been quiet this whole time barked at Lars and lunged, extending the chain as far as it would go. Lars tilted his head at Duke, who continued to growl and bark and yank on the chain.

"Who's a tough doggy, huh?" he said to Duke in a sing-song tone. "Are you gonna get me?" He leaned in and Duke lunged at him again. Lars stepped closer. "Who's a tough doggy? You are! Yes, you are!" Lars leaned in real close. Duke leaped out, but Lars was too fast and jumped back. He repeated these taunts, jumping back and flinging both arms up mockingly, almost in a peekaboo fashion, baiting Duke.

Once again, Jayden gripped the lottery rock in his coat pocket, noting the rhythm of Lars's taunts. On the fourth taunt, Jayden hurled the rock at Lars and hit the hand holding the revolver. When the gun clattered to the ground, Jayden dived, but his hand knocked the firearm, spinning it around in circles on the stone floor. Scrambling to his knees, he grabbed for the gun and bumped it into Lars's foot. Lars reflexively kicked out, sending it off the cliff's edge.

"You motherfucker!" Lars pounced on Jayden like a mountain lion.

Wide-eyed, Duke frothed, growled, and barked, stretching his chain as far as it would go.

Firmly pinned beneath Lars's tight grip, Jayden tried kicking him with his legs but couldn't get them to budge. The asshole had him good.

"Duke!" Jayden yelled. "Help!"

He felt his head knock against the stone ground before Lars pulled his fist back for another punch. After the second hit, Jayden's world went dizzy.

"I'm gonna kill you first, and then torture your fucking dog."

Lars reached for his belt and unsheathed a hunting knife.

A shrill piercing cry echoed from the canyon below, causing Lars to lift his head. With his hair hanging past his face, his eyes widened. He grinned.

"It's time."

A much louder screech tore through the night air.

Jayden swallowed.

With the stealth of a night owl, the Crenlin Devil landed on Satan's Perch. Lars's eyes widened in surprise and his razor thin smile dimpled his cheeks. He glanced at the beast.

"You finally showed up," Lars said, raising his knife above his head. "Let the sacrifice begin."

At the weapon's apex, the blade glinted in the moon's light. Jayden could feel the hard ground, hear his dog barking like crazy, and understood in this instant of time that his life hung in the balance of a blade.

Freeing his arm, he caught the downward jab of the knife on the bone of his wrist. A sharp sting. Hot blood. Not even thinking, he blocked another knife jab with the edge of his palm. Blood splattered his face. He went to block again but the blade froze in the air as Lars pulled back on his haunches.

The winged demon's sharp talons thumped the ground next to Jayden. Its black eyes now so close that the puff of air from its nostrils blew Jayden's hair back. The monster's lips curled, exposing dark black fangs before it released a low guttural growl that rumbled Jayden's core. He expected death by either the Crenlin Devil or Lars. The Crenlin Devil moved its nostrils up to Jayden's ripped jacket sleeve. While it sniffed the blood, Lars let out a wicked laugh, raising the hunting knife higher.

A single whap from the beast's snout knocked Lars off Jayden, hurling him to the side and almost over the cliff. In one leap, the beast pinned Lars and bore its black eyes into him.

"No!" Lars shook his head back and forth while the beast's sable stare turned a glowing red to plumb the depths of the creep's mind. "Please don't!"

Clutching Lars in its talons, the beast lunged off the ground. A gust of wind and dust hit Jayden in the face. Lars squirmed and yelled as the Crenlin Devil sliced its wings through the darkness. Within seconds, the beast's silhouette soared high into the sky.

Now sitting up on his elbows, Jayden held his breath.

The owl from earlier hooted again in the quiet night.

The Crenlin Devil released. Screaming, Lars fell through the air and dropped into the canyon. Jayden exhaled, counting the seconds it would take Lars to hit the ground, one, two, three . . . Still dizzy, he crawled to the edge of Satan's Perch expecting to see Brody's dark blue coat or a blob that represented Lars. But there was only darkness and a roaring river that must have swept them both away. Curling into a ball, a wave of gut-wrenching sorrow made Jayden consider rolling into the ravine to join his friend.

"Brody," he said aloud. His body convulsing in sobs. "Brody, I'm sorry."

Duke's chain rattled.

"Sorry," Jayden said again.

"For what?"

The voice, so clear. Imagined. But real sounding.

He uncurled, rolled over, and pulled himself up to see Brody kneeling next to Duke. He'd heard once that concussions could cause hallucinations, but the ghost of Brody was so real.

"I'm okay." Brody smiled.

Jayden steadied himself then shuffled over and embraced Brody only to bawl some more.

"I'm okay. I swear." Brody hugged back. "But you look like shit."

With his chin resting on Brody's shoulder, Jayden asked, "How'd you survive a fall like that?"

"Yeah, right? Of all the crazy ass things in this world, I'm saved by the Crenlin Devil."

Jayden sniffled and embraced harder to prove he was hugging a real person and not a ghost.

"And you came back for me." Jayden let go of the embrace.

"Of course I came back for you." Brody reached up and Jayden winced when he touched the bruise on his cheekbone. "That hit scrambled your brains, didn't it?"

Brody thought Jayden lost his mind. "No, I meant, how'd you know it was safe?"

"Because the Crenlin Devil wouldn't save me only to drop you from the sky."

"Huh." Jayden nodded, plopped down next to Duke, and squeezed him. "True."

All three sat for a moment, mostly so Jayden, who now clenched his hand to his chest to stop the bleeding, could regain his bearings. A breeze swayed the branches sounding like Duke's nails clicking on the linoleum floor at home. His dog rested his muzzle on Jayden's lap in a concerned whine and huff.

"I'm okay, boy," Jayden said. The Crenlin Devil passed by the moon before swooping down and out of sight into the canyon. Both boys pushed off the ground to head home. Brody held Duke's chain while Jayden held his injured arm.

"Your brother was wrong," Jayden said.

Brody scrunched up his eyes. "Huh?"

"Monsters aren't beasts born from darkness and pure evil." The thought that now rattled around in Jayden's head scared him more than any creature in a nightmare or movie. He looked at Brody. "Monsters are human."

Retired Honor

Richard M. Hamp

SIR BROCADE, KNIGHT of the realm of Furborn and paladin of the Platinum Acorn Guard, winced at the bouncing of his heavy charger as it clomped down the road. The squirrel knight dropped a delicate gray paw onto the bandage tightly wound around his knee. The bandage was soaked through with both blood and the incessant rain that they had traveled through for most of the day. Though the wound would mend with time and rest as all the others had, the knight was fairly certain that he would have a bald patch from where the spear had grazed him. Fur was a point of pride for squirrel folk and to have patchy fur… well, he supposed he had other things to be proud of and it was unlikely that anyone would dare criticize a fully armed and armored knight to their face, at least.

A few other scars showed through the thin fur on his face and arms, but most were hidden well enough by his warm silvery-colored fur. Something deeper than a graze cut him this last battle and it had nothing to do with the wound under the bandage. Sir Brocade was pensive and distant and his squire, Gidzo, seemed to sense it, remaining quieter than usual for the boisterous lizard.

"Does it still pain ya overly much, Master Brocade?" Gidzo's blue and orange-spotted scales glistened in the early-morning light as the squire looked up from where he kept pace alongside Sir Brocade's horse. The lizard's long fleshy tongue slurped up and moistened an eye while watching his knight.

"Only when this unsympathetic nag of a horse sees fit to bounce me around like a sack of cabbages. Hear that, girl? Gentler." The knight patted the horse's neck. "Turn the beast into glue before long." The horse whinnied in reply.

"Oh, now, sir. That won't do at all. She's been seein' you safely into and out of battles for long as I've been with you. Just cause she's a hoofie and can't talk back ain't no reason to disrespect her. That there's a good beast. And one what puts up with your armor lookin' and, like as not, smellin' a mess. I wish you'd let us stop so I could give it a good wash and oil. You don't look much like a knight of Furborn right now. More a vagrant of Underbelly. Sir Underbelly, I should call you."

"Gidzo!" Sir Brocade laughed. "I'm your master. You can't talk to me like that."

The lizard gave a half-cocked smile that spanned a full half of his speckled head. “Can talk any ways I see fit long as I got the map and you don’t.” He patted a rolled up oiled parchment in his dark leather satchel. “Not that me map would be helpin’ you over much. Got my own doubts that you could find your way out of a privy without me pointin’ out the door.”

The squirrel laughed and kicked out at his squire playfully with his good leg. The gecko darted aside to avoid it easily. “That’s it, disrespectful gecko! You’re released from your position. You’ll receive no recommendation from me either. Though that can wait until we reach the next civilized area where I can hire a guide.”

“A course, sir,” Gidzo said, patting the knight’s leg in mocking sympathy. “Wouldn’t dream of abandonin’ you to the dangers of this here dirt road after you were kind enough to fire me and all.”

The squire was right about the knight’s appearance, though. Sir Brocade’s gold-gilded armor was covered in the blood and mud and desperation of their most recent battle. If the fight could have been called a battle. The opposing side had been mostly peasants pressed into the service. Most of the mice and dog soldiers hadn’t even had proper weapons, just pitchforks or makeshift spears. Appearances be damned, let his armor stay dirty. That fight had left a poor feeling in his soul.

Sir Brocade had, once again, had accolades and pronouncements of his courage and acumen in battle heaped upon him after the fighting was done. He received yet another shiny silver medal for killing people who should have been in fields of corn and barley instead of a field of battle. He'd had Gidzo throw it into the chest along with all the dozens of others.

Gidzo wrung his clawed hands, the vertical pupil of his yellow eyes cast toward the ground. He was always like this when he was worried about something. The squirrel took a deep breath in an attempt to clear away the dark thoughts. He had better make peace with them quickly, he was fairly certain he was to be called out again within the month for yet another skirmish up north.

"Out with it, Gidzo. You are a most noble gecko and a squire of the realm. It does not behoove you to be so sheepish with your thoughts. No offense to sheep, of course. Fine friends and stalwart allies on the field of battle." Gidzo had been a constant companion of the squirrel knight for nearly five years now and a full squire for three of those. The gecko was more than a simple squire to Brocade, the relationship was far deeper than that.

"If you don't mind me sayin' sir, you seem a bit off." Gidzo's bulbous tongue slicked out of his mouth and licked the scales around his lips whether to further moisten them or slurp up the rain, Sir Brocade wasn't certain. "Not like meat left out too long or nothin', but like yer thinkin' deep, profound-like thoughts."

The squirrel brushed his arm across his face to clear the rain slick off, only managing to wipe muck from his fur across his nose. "I suppose I am." Killing was in his blood, but he couldn't help but wonder if there was anything else worthwhile still in his veins. He looked around at the fields and woods around them. Beautiful country. "Tell me, Gidzo, have we passed this way before?"

"No, sir." The gecko pulled the large map out of his pack and unrolled it while he walked, hunching over the parchment in an attempt to keep most of the misty rain off. The lizard stretched it out with both hands and used his tail to point to a faint gray squiggle of a path amidst the dark black lines that showed the king's highways. "You said you were wantin' to be off the beaten track. So, we're using this one here." He pointed to the faintest of the lines on the map, barely visible from where Sir Brocade sat atop his mount. "Don't even got no name, just a bit o' packed dirt between villages."

They passed an area with a dark forest on one side and an overgrown field on the other. A sad, gray house squatted in the middle of the field. Its roof sagged and both front windows were broken out. A single willow tree, leaning to one side as though it was struggling against the wind, grew not far from the path itself. A homestead that hadn't been a home to anyone in a very long time.

A wooden sign with painted letters worn away by wind and rain was nailed to the tree and read: *Make Offer at Stone and Song Tavern.*

"Gidzo, what is the next village we will come to?"

"Havenbrook, sir. Just a bit over a mile up the road here. T'aint nothin' really." The lizard scoured his map. "Just a dot in the middle o' everythin' more important."

"Just a dot, eh?" The squirrel rubbed his chin and continued to look at the sign as they continued toward Havenbrook. "Do you think we should stop at the tavern?"

The gecko's scaled face turned up into a wide smile. "Yeah. We sure should at that, sir master knight, sir. My feet could use a rest and throat could use a drink."

The small, well-kept tavern had at least a dozen locals all sharing drinks and laughing with one another. Gidzo took to it immediately and was singing some tavern song with the patrons within the hour. A possum named Starcy shooed several children who were ogling the knight's armor away to clean and rewrap his wound. Knight and squire laughed and drank well into the night and Sir Brocade felt for maybe the first time that he was more than just his sword.

"Gidzo," the squirrel said, eyes blurry from the drinks. "I would like to rest in Havenbrook a bit longer."

The gecko smiled knowingly. "Thought you might, sir. Was just waitin' on you to figure out what I already knew. Pidge, that's the cat behind the bar there, said she'd sell that homestead we passed off for one of your silver medals. Got a few sons that'll help mend the fences and barn for one more."

It was the morning after the barn was finished that Sir Brocade and Gidzo dug a deep hole at the base of the willow tree in the front yard. The knight carefully packed away the armor and sword, wrapping them in a white wool blanket and enclosing them in a stout ironbound chest. Without a word, they lowered the chest.

The squirrel put his paw on his chest while looking into the hole. "I swear on my honor, I will touch neither armor nor arms for any king or prince again. Nor shall I be known as a knight or warrior. I will take my mother's surname and be known simply as Tails." With that, the great knight, Sir Brocade, was buried under the willow tree along with his arms and armaments and Mr. Tails was born.

"It be them brigands again, mark me," Gidzo said as the old lizard pulled weeds from around the tomato plants. The tinker hadn't come for the past two months to sharpen knives or mend pots and Gidzo had the habit of blaming everything that happened around the town of Havenbrook on the local collection of highwaymen. Though this time, thought Tails as he puffed at his long pipe with his back against the willow, the lizard might have a point. Besides, Tails' crochet needle had been stepped on and either a repair or new needle was in order. Either way, that took a skilled tinker.

The years had been kind to them both, full of life and love. When they had finally become accustomed to being equals instead of knight and squire, the dynamic of their relationship took a surprising turn. At least, it was surprising for Tails who had never thought of Gidzo as anything other than a squire and friend up to that point—certainly not a husband.

"Mr. Gidzo," Tomney, one of the local dog pups from the next farm over who came by to help with the more strenuous chores these days, ran up, his shock of blond hair erupting from his skull in seemingly random directions. Though, Tails had to admit, he was becoming less of a pup and more of a dog by day. He'd be ready to start his own family within the next few years. "I'm done feeding the animals and mucking the stables. Is that all you needed today?" The pup's tail poked out from the hole in his overalls and thumped against the side of the elevated planter Gidzo was working in. The arthritic lizard winced with each "thump".

"Yeah, Tomney." Gidzo stood upright, placing the shovel he had been using next to the bed and reached around to rub his back. His scales had dulled from the vibrant orange and blue of youth to more pastel colors these days, but Tails still thought the gecko one of the most beautiful things in the world. "That layabout husband of mine will have your copper penny."

The squirrel's former experiences as a knight hadn't prepared him for farming life and he turned out to be a very poor hand at it. Gidzo, on the other hand, fell to it with ease and managed to keep the property running smoothly despite Tails' best efforts, which mostly ended up costing more time and money than if the squirrel had stayed out of it in the first place.

Luckily, knighthood had been lucrative, and he had come into this new life with a bag full of silver medals to melt down or trade off as needed. At least his money had been useful.

Tomney ran up—Tails was convinced the pup never learned to actually walk, just took off at a dead run the moment his feet started working. “Mr. Tails, Mr. Gidzo said—”

Tails chuckled behind his large incisors. “Yeah, Tomney, he’s a dozen feet away. I heard. I’m not quite that deaf yet.” He dug around in a pouch at his side.

“Do you know if Mr. Gidzo is going to tell stories about Sir Brocade at the Tavern tonight? My parents said the new litter is finally old enough for Nan to watch and we can go next time.”

Gidzo had been telling stories at the tavern for years. The children listened to Gidzo spin tales of the daring and valiant Sir Brocade—a knight who had disappeared suddenly from the realm—while the grandparents who remembered Tails as he was cast sly glances. But they kept the secret well enough. In this way, the years had grown softer and Tails was very much enjoying his golden years lazing in the sun and listening to his love spin increasingly outlandish stories about Sir Brocade. Stories which everyone in the town had heard at least three or four times. Tails had requested Gidzo change the name of his favorite protagonist as the stories didn’t even resemble reality any longer, but the lizard insisted it was more fun when the hero was sitting unbeknownst among everyone listening.

The conversation was interrupted by a pair of horsemen coming down the road. One was a large beaver with stark yellow teeth, the other a squat porcupine. Both wore thick, iron-ringed armor with well-handled war axes at their belts. Their tabards bore the crossed tree heraldry of the monarchy. Tomney gasped. Gidzo gave a brief curse and threw down a handful of wilted leaves he'd been plucking.

"Hey-O, gents," the gecko said, raising one arm. "What're you abouts?"

The beaver looked down his nose at the gecko and slapped his horse with a wide, flat tail, stopping the beast instantly.

"Our lord has heard," the beaver spoke with lisping s's, "that a missing knight may be in the vicinity. A traitor to the crown and most dishonorable animal who abandoned his duties."

"He's soundin' terrible." Gidzo scratched at his scales with one claw. "You got a name for the scoundrel to go with that fancy description of character?"

The porcupine bristled at the gecko's tone and squeaked out. "Respect, green thing, lest I give you a closer look at my quills!"

Tails reached over and grabbed his cane. A lackluster weapon against two armored and powerful opponents, but perhaps something of the old skills were still there.

"Peace there, friends," Gidzo opened his arms as though to show he meant no harm. "No offense intended. Just lookin' for the name. Ain't heard of no knight round here."

The beaver hunched down, the iron rings of his armor jingling. "Sir Broken."

"Brocade," the porcupine whispered. The correction wasn't lost on Tails.

"Brocade," the beaver corrected and seemed to take notice of Tails for the first time. "A squirrel knight. Would be an old squirrel by now, if not dead. But stories have come to our lord's ears that talk of just such a knight has been coming from these parts."

Tails risked a glance over to Tomney. The pup stood tall. His tail was slightly tucked, but he wasn't cowed by the two soldiers in front of them. The squirrel smiled. That pup had some mettle to him.

"Something funny, squirrel?" the porcupine demanded.

"Actually, yes. I do believe I'm the only squirrel living in this area. I was chuckling at the idea that I was this Sir Broken—"

"Brocade!"

"Of course. Apologies. Sir *Brocade.*" He heaved himself to his feet, leaning slightly more heavily than usual on his cane. He patted some of the dust off of his overalls and put a finger through one of several holes in his flannel shirt. "Have slopping animals and fertilizing gardens with manure become virtues of the knighthood? If so, I'm quite the model."

Gidzo motioned toward Tails. "Last time he so much as looked at one of them buckets of manure, much less toted one around, was when you boys was still playing with wooden swords in nappies."

Tails chuckled. "I'm just trying to make a point here, my love."

"Well, I'd say your virtues are layin' about under the shade or in the sun dependin' on how the weather is treatin' your bones. Mayhaps that's knightly."

The two soldiers snorted down at them and wheeled their steeds around, continuing down the road. This had happened occasionally. But something was different about these two. They didn't wear the armor as comfortably as soldiers accustomed to it.

Tails brushed off the thought and pulled a coin out of his pouch, sliding it into Tomney's paw. "Hope that didn't startle you too much, lad."

"Nah. They come by our farm every few years, too. I think it's because Mr. Gidzo talks about Sir Brocade in all his stories." The pup stopped and looked directly at Tails. "Did you ever know him the way Mr. Gidzo did?"

Tails smiled. Tomney's grandparents were among the first to welcome him and Gidzo to the valley. They had known very well who he had been. "I met him a time or two, but am not half the storyteller my husband is."

Tomney looked down at the coin in his hand. "Oh, sir. You've made a mistake. This is a silver penny, not a copper one."

"Well then, you best put it in your pocket before I notice," Tails replied. "Buy your family a meal at the tavern tonight. The curmudgeonly lizard will be there."

Tomney's snout broke out into a wide smile, his tongue lolling out the side of his mouth. "Thank you, sir. I will! Oh, wow!" And the pup sprinted back toward his family's farm, legs kicking up dust on the road as they churned.

"I see I get no say so about what I'm doin' these days," Gidzo complained. "What if I wasn't plannin' on goin' to the tavern tonight, eh? What if I was goin' to . . . ?" the gecko trailed off.

"Continue, please." Tails prodded. "What else were you planning on doing this evening? Sit at home and relish that you're disappointing the local children by not being at the tavern?"

"Mayhaps I was goin' to be countin' out how much coin yer wastin' givin' silver out to the boys we hire for copper. We'll be broke before midwinter, mark me."

"Yes, yes. Well, I'll still love you when you're shaking a tin cup for alms," Tails said.

Gidzo huffed and looked away, but not fast enough to hide his smile.

They still had a handful of silver medals left in the lockbox and, between those and renting out the farmland they had both spent years pulling rocks out of, they should be comfortable for the remainder of their days. Tomney's family, however, just had another litter of pups and could use the extra coin.

"Damn," Gidzo said, looking into the seed pouch. "I done forgot to buy basil seeds from Moriganne. Ain't no use tryin' to get tomatoes without basil next to 'em. Sad, shriveled things they'd be." He stood up and rubbed his lower back again. "Well, nothin' done without startin'. Mayhaps I can wave at our friendly soldier boys in town."

Tails grabbed his cane and used it to help himself to his feet. "Nonsense. Stay here and get a hot water bottle on that back. You've gotten old, lizard, whereas I am still young and spry." The squirrel winked as he massaged the left knee that had been hurting him for a couple of years. "I'll get the seed."

The gecko licked his eye as he always did while thinking. "If I let you go, I'll have to hear about your knee hurtin' for days. You go mind dinner. I'll get another bag of flour and some of that moisturizing balm. I think I'm about to molt."

Tails laughed outright. "Wishful thinking. You haven't molted in a decade, but you get your balm."

"I'm gonna buy a pound of honey snaps from Moriganne, too."

The squirrel cocked an eyebrow.

"Now you be stoppin' that." A scaled hand pointed at the offending eyebrow. "Got all the garden done t'day, no thanks to the squirrel that just lays about smoking in the shade, relaxing the day away. I can damn sure have some candy if'n I want."

Tails smiled and leaned in to kiss Gidzo's scaley cheek. "Be back in an hour with your candy." He turned and walked toward the house.

Tails went inside to start dinner and put in a speckled meat pie. He then settled down with the crocheted mittens he was trying his best to get done before winter for Gidzo. He had only just learned how to crochet with the largest hooked needle the tinker carried this last summer. And he wasn't very good at all. The squirrel could link a straight line of woolen yarn and have that straight line connect to another one but struggled with anything beyond that. Crochet was more complicated than swordplay.

An hour turned to two. Tails took the pie out of the oven to cool and dampened the fire below. Moriganne must have gotten to talking as she was wont to do. The mittens were coming along nicely even if the squirrel had to undo a row for every two he managed to keep. He should get it done before cooler weather settled into the area.

Two hours turned to three and afternoon started to wane. Moriganne chatting wouldn't have delayed Gidzo so long; perhaps he was coaxed into telling a story before the dinner rush was over and everyone at the tavern settled in for an evening's relaxation. Tails poured himself a couple fingers of bourbon before setting about to make a simple syrup for cocktails. It was getting chillier and the gecko had only taken his light jacket—he might need something to warm him up when he returned.

Three hours stretched out until the sun hung low in a red sky. Nothing should have taken the lizard this long without sending word. Havenbrook was only a bit over a mile away. Tails pulled his boots on and grabbed his ebony cane and coat. He paused on the way out the door to grab a thick scarf for when he found the wayward lizard.

The trail was, thankfully, quite dry as Tails walked as quickly as his knee would allow. Trees lined both sides of the path, but they were as familiar and known as old friends along with the ruts in the dirt. Despite its familiarity and proximity to town, however, something ominous seemed to press in on the closing moments of daylight.

Midway to Havenbrook, he found Gidzo. The old lizard was lying on the road, a trail of blood behind him from where he had tried to crawl home. The well-worn leather satchel he carried his coin in was missing and there was an ugly gash in his head.

"Gidzo!" Tails shouted, dropping to the lizard's side. His knee screamed in pain, but the squirrel ignored it. The lizard lay still in the dirt, cold but breathing shallowly.

Tails pulled at his own linen shirt, trying to rip a strip off to bind the wound as he had done so many times on the battlefield, but after straining and failing to pull the cloth apart, he finally had to snatch the small knife Gidzo kept at his belt to cut a piece off and wrap around the lizard's head. The wrap soaked through almost immediately. Biting his lip against tears, the squirrel wrapped the scarf he had brought around his husband's cold body before hefting it, feeling a slight shuddering breath from the cold gecko as he picked him up. Lying on the ground for so long had drained the lizard of all warmth. Tails wrapped his tail around this precious cargo and shuffled down the road to Havenbrook, arms and legs strengthened by desperation. Body aching from the unaccustomed exertion, Tails focused on placing one foot in front of the other. The town would normally only be ten or fifteen minutes away, and Tails needed to get help for Gidzo immediately. If not, the gecko might—

He felt himself getting choked up as thoughts of his companion dying raced through his head. He just needed to get to town. It wasn't far. Minutes crawled by as slowly as the squirrel's limping footsteps. Finally, he stumbled into the familiarity of Havenbrook and felt the energy of desperation drain from his body.

"Tails!" Tomney shouted and gave a friendly wave from the front of the Stone and Song Tavern, where the pup was obviously waiting with the rest of his family for the evening stories to begin. The young hound must have seen something was wrong as his ears perked up and the grin faded into concern. Tomney leaped off the tavern porch and raced down the street ahead of his father in a ruddy-colored blur.

"Help." Tails gasped and collapsed to the ground, trying to cushion the lizard's fall into the dirt with his tail as much as possible. He wasn't certain if Gidzo was still breathing—he hadn't dared to check on the way. The squirrel struggled to stand back up, to get his companion to help, but his legs wouldn't obey and refused to carry even his own weight any farther. He lay on the ground, eyes on the green skin of the lizard he loved, dust coating his lips and black nose.

"I got him, Mr. Tails." And a weight was lifted from him. Tomney's strong arms effortlessly carried the limp lizard. A half second later, other warm paws were lifting Tails up and helping him limp down the street. Within a few stumbling steps, dozens of townsfolk were surrounding the two old friends who always came to tell stories after the week's work was done.

Moriganne, the plump mole who ran the general store pushed through to Tails' side.

"What happened here, Tails?" Her voice was drawn out like a slow mandolin song. "I just saw the rascal a few hours ago. Bought me out of candy and complimented my dress."

"I found him like that on the trail," Tails panted as he was half-carried to the tavern. He took a shaking breath as they pushed into the smoky interior. It was a crowded weekend evening with most of the town pressed into the space to catch up with friends or hear Gidzo's outlandish stories. The two king's guards, still in their shirts of thick iron rings and carrying short axes sat at a back table, adding to the crowded space. Strange they'd still be in armor.

Gentle paws cleared off one of the tables and laid Gidzo on it. Dace, the coyote owner of Stone and Song, washed her hands quickly before scurrying from behind the bar to attend to the gecko. The coyote had been a medic before she retired to open the tavern; Tails remembered her from several battles, though they'd never spoken of it. She remembered her craft well when it concerned children with scraped knees and bee stings. He prayed her knowledge still extended beyond that.

"He was so late coming home," Tails said. Someone pushed a mug of water in his hand, but he didn't pay it any mind. "I went to search."

"Damnable brigands." Jacoby, Tomney's father, growled low. Other growls echoed his sentiment from the townsfolk. "They're too close to the town. We'll need to round up a group to go smoke them out."

Moriganne pulled up a chair for Tails and he allowed himself to be sat down next to Gidzo. He reached out and took his companion's hand, gently brushing his thumb against the thin, cold, scaled skin of the gecko's arm. Dace went about her business, pulling off Gidzo's shirt to check his chest and arms. Tails clenched his eyes against the tears at seeing the deep purple bruises across the lizard's shoulder where the satchel was slung.

"Hey! We was eating!" The gruff lisping voice of the beaver complained as the locals cleared off a table to get the semi-clean cloth underneath. The pair of kingdom soldiers looked offended as their table was disrupted and their evening meal thrown haphazardly onto the long bar. No one paid them any mind other than Tails, who sat staring at the porcupine's ripped tabard. No king's soldier would have left it like that. The first thing they would have done in town was have a rip mended. Unfitted armor, ripped clothing, blood splatters. These weren't king's soldiers. These were brigands masquerading!

Rage pounded within the squirrel's head, making his eardrums throb. He struggled up, his legs shaking with the effort, still staring at the heavily armed pair as they grinned and dribbled mead across their furry faces and drank. He dropped Gidzo's hand and plucked a butter knife off a nearby table. It wasn't much against the stolen axes, but if he could surprise the first one and then duck under just one swing, the armor at the porcupine's armpit would be exposed and he could—

"Oh, what are you about now, squirrel?" The beaver said, standing up at Tails' approach, his paw fingering the axe at his belt. "Stand back from the king's soldiers."

"You're fake," Tails hissed. "You did this!" He was still ready to pounce, old training informing his body. The two fake soldiers stood up and drew their weapons, more than ready for an old squirrel. Then a soft paw pressed him back.

"Mr. Tails," Tomney said, pushing the squirrel steadily back. "They got armor on and axes. They'll kill you and that won't help Mr. Gidzo any. I don't know what is going on, but you can't fight them now."

Anger flooded through Tails. "Not like this I can't." And the squirrel pushed through the questioning townsfolk, stopping only to give Gidzo's hand a squeeze, before venturing out into the night once again.

"This mean we ain't getting story time in there tonight?" The porcupine laughed from behind Tails.

His trip back to the farm was quickened by rage. The moon was just bright enough to find his way along the path through the dark trees. Tails refused to allow his knee to be an impediment to what needed to be done despite how it throbbed under the long strides that ate up the distance. Fury would see him through this last battle.

Tails saw the light from the lantern he'd left burning in the window before the farm came clear from out of the night's darkness. The long hanging strands of the willow tree swayed darkly in the moonlit farm as though trying to wave off the furious squirrel. Tails paid no mind while grabbing the shovel Gidzo had been using to remove weeds from between the tomato plants just hours earlier. He plunged the spade into the dirt below the willow tree. Throwing dirt into the darkness of the night around him, oblivious to where it might land. All he cared about in the moment was retrieving what he needed to exert justice on those who had hurt his family. But his aging body was not accustomed to the brutal exertion he had already forced upon it and after the hole was several hands deep, his frantic digging slowed.

He pushed through the aching in his arms and back, willing each shovel full of dirt out of the hole past the sweat and burning muscles. It took over an hour of digging before his spade thunked against the top of the chest buried so long ago. He cleared off the top before collapsing into the dirt. He lay gasping at the bottom of the hole covered in sweat and dirt and despair. It took so long to get even this far; he still needed to don his armor and get back to town.

Tails heard feet crunching on the path to the house. A moment later a familiar silhouette peeked over the lip of the hole and a voice broke the night. "So, you can still be puttin' in a day's work when there's motivation nuf." A swollen-faced but smiling gecko stared down into the hole.

The squirrel's jaw worked up and down without words coming.

"Dace knows her craft, both at the bar and with a bandage. Just needed a bit o' rest next to the fire to warm my cold blood up. Course, you was gone already. Figured out what you may be up to pretty quick. Jacoby lent me a ride on their wagon with a few others to get out here 'fore you did somethin' truly stupid. As is your wont."

Tails turned back toward the chest lid, uncovered and ready to be opened. "I can't let them get away with it. You were hurt so bad. They'll just come back and do it again to you or someone else."

"Tails." Gidzo's swollen face became serious as he reached his hand toward the squirrel's paw. "You've been my husband for decades and my best friend for near the whole of my life. I love you more than anythin'. Leave that lid closed and that other fellow buried. You ain't him anymore and we don't need you to be."

The squirrel wiped the tears from his eyes with his soiled tail and nodded, accepting the reaching hand and clambering out of the hole. "You're right. He should remain buried."

"There now, love," Gidzo said, wrapping his green arms around the openly weeping squirrel.

Tails sniffed. "We have to tell the town about those two, at least. Get a local constable or—"

"Shush now. All that's been taken care of." He motioned toward the wagon. The two thugs were bloodied and bound in the back with several of the townsfolk, including Tomney standing and holding a table leg menacingly over them.

"That pup we've had helpin' us out got pretty attached to us, seems to me. Soon as you stormed out, he got a gang of townsfolk together and they gave those two a right good beatin'. They are gonna take a trip to turn 'em over to the authorities tomorrow."

Tails reached over and held the hand of Gidzo before glancing over his shoulder down at the hole he had dug in his anger.

"You were right. I shouldn't have dug him up. I'll fill the hole back in tomorrow," the squirrel said.

"Course I was right. And what's this nonsense about you filling it in?" Gidzo gently turned them both toward the house. "You'll be bedridden and whining about how sore you are well into next week with all the running around and digging you did today. I'll be the one filling it in."

The pair shuffled across the porch and into their home.

The gecko pulled shut the door behind them. “Though, thinkin’ about it, mayhaps we just overpay Tomney to do it when he gets back while we sit under the tree and eat honey snaps.”

About the Authors

Caitlin Berve is an award-winning fantasy author, editor, and speaker. Through Ignited Ink Writing, she edits novels, creates video tutorials, and writes. Her CIPA EVVY winning collection of modern fairy tales *When Magic Calls* is available in paperback, ebook, and audiobook formats. Caitlin seeks to fill the world with the kind of writing that lingers with readers and to find magic in modern times. For more fantasy stories by Caitlin, go to **caitlinberve.com.** For her writing advice and editing services, go to **ignitedinkwriting.com**.

Laura Blegen is a bookkeeper and author, who grew up in the Midwest and now lives on the edge of the Colorado Rocky Mountains. She and her husband have two cats, and a shared propensity for taking off on ridiculous adventures.

Richard M. Hamp writes silly stories that some at 30th Street Fiction have called "not completely unsuccessful". When not basking in the praise of his peers, he irradiates insects and arachnids with a low-voltage microwave in hopes of becoming a Marvel hero. He's gotten a few cortisol shots to help the swelling from the bites go down, but no superpowers yet. One can never abandon hope, though. You can find him at **richardhamp.com**.

Lezly Harrison is a retired computer programmer who fills her time writing, painting, and hiking the trails of Boulder, Colorado.

Jon Logan Hart works in tech and writes science fiction, horror, and erotica.

Kate Jonuska is a writer of fiction, features, and F-bombs whose short stories are Pushcart Prize-nominated and whose first novel, *Transference*, was a finalist for the 2017 BookLife Prize. She also wrote *The Dictionary of Fiction Critique*, teaches yoga, and is making something delicious for dinner tonight. Details at **katejonuska.com**.

Jessica Lavé is a writer living in the Denver area in Colorado. When procrastinating on her word count, she enjoys baking pies, watching true crime and crime fiction series, playing fetch with her cat or visiting local breweries with her dog. Find more about the author at **jessicalave.com**.

Ian K. Long is a writer based in Boulder, Colorado. Find him online at **PenAndIchor.com**.

Juliana Rew is a software engineer and former science and technical writer for the National Center for Atmospheric Research in Boulder, Colorado. She has published stories in *The Colored Lens*, *Stupefying Stories*, *PerihelionSF*, and *Mad Scientist Journal*, among others. She is the author of the science fiction novel, *The Unwinding: Gin's Story*, as well as two YA SFF series. Her author website is **julianarew.com.**

About the Authors

About 30th Street Fiction

Based in Boulder, Colorado, 30th Street Fiction is an established critique group and supportive community of writers who meet bi-monthly to swap snarky comments, bad advice, and the occasional critique of our fellow writers' fiction. As **30th Street Press**, the group works to publish and promote independently published fiction. Their first book, *Proof: A 30th Street Fiction Anthology,* was published in 2017, their second, *Flight: A 30th Street Fiction Anthology,* in 2019, and their third anthology, *Broken: A 30th Street Fiction Anthology,* was released in 2021. Learn more at **30thstreetpress.com**.

Made in the USA
Monee, IL
13 May 2025

17352558R10111